DARK ABANDON

THE ARONDIGHT CODEX - BOOK THREE

NICOLE R. TAYLOR

Dark Abandon (The Arondight Codex - Book Three) by
Nicole R. Taylor

Copyright © 2019 by Nicole R. Taylor

All rights reserved.

No part of this book may be reproduced in any form or by any
electronic or mechanical means, including information storage and
retrieval systems, without written permission from the author, except
for the use of brief quotations in a book review.

www.nicolertaylorwrites.com

Cover Design: Covers by Juan

Edited by: Silvia Curry

PROLOGUE

"I think we're safe for now."

Mea glanced up at the sound of Chris's voice and heaved a sigh of relief. They'd been on the move for the past week, barely evading detection. It was a relief to stand still, even if it was only for a day or two.

Chris had a formidable presence, and even now, it filled the tiny kitchen to the brim. At six-foot-four, he stood a whole head and shoulders over her, and that wasn't including the hard muscle that he'd built up over the years of training as a Natural.

She had much of the same experiences at the London Sanctum, but Mea was more athletic. Weaving Light was more suited to her strengths, while Chris' was brute force. Together, they made the perfect pair. She supposed that's why they ended up together.

"How is she?" he asked, making sure the door was locked.

"She's fine. Happy even." Mea threw a glance at the toddler sitting on the rug. She was a pretty child, even if she was a little different with her purple-tinted hair. It was only a hint, but as she grew, it'd become brighter. "You know Scarlett. Nothing worries her."

"Good. I think we'll be okay to stay here tonight. I'll reassess in the morning."

"I haven't felt anything for hours, not since we left Bristol."

Chris frowned and sat beside her at the kitchen table. "We've been careful. We can take a breath, but I want to keep moving."

"Can't we stay for a little while?" Exhaustion—both mental and physical—was catching up with her. It was messing with her Light and without it, she couldn't sense the Dark as well as she ought to.

"We must keep her safe," he replied, glancing at the girl. "She's our only hope."

"One more night."

"They're closing in on us, Mea. We're running out of places to hide."

She looked across the kitchen to where Scarlett was playing with a set of battered building blocks. Barely three, the little girl was already making complex shapes and designs. Her vocabulary was accelerating, too. Just the day before, she'd called Mea ludicrous… and knew exactly what it meant.

"It's not fair," she murmured. "She's got so much weight on her shoulders, and she's barely begun to live."

"Life isn't meant to be fair," Chris said, "it's natural selection."

She understood. They were all a part of something bigger than themselves, but sacrificing everything they'd ever known—family, friends, and their own kind—for the greater good, took a toll. Scarlett would never know a normal life. She'd never go to school, have friends, a boyfriend, get married, or have children. If everything went according to Gilhana's plan, then—

"I can't bear it, Chris." She let her head fall into her hands.

"We both chose to make this sacrifice," he said as he rubbed soothing circles on her back. "We both knew it might come down to this."

"I know," she whispered. "It's just… Some days are harder than others."

He nodded and wrapped his arms around her. "Knowing what might happen to her never gets any easier. In anther time and place, we may not have even met her. If this is how it ends, then we die knowing we did all we could to protect the Flame."

"I know we need to trust Gilhana, but—"

"Shh," Chris soothed. "I know she's crazy as shite on a stick, but she's a Druid, Mea."

Cold air tugged at her fingertips and she sucked in a sharp breath, her head snapping up.

Chris stiffened, automatically reaching for his arondight blade. "What is it?"

"Darkness…" she rasped. "They're here. They—"

"Quick." He stood to his feet and began to check

all the windows, peering at the street outside. Every time he pulled back a blind, orange light spilled into the flat. "*Shite*. They're coming."

He didn't have to explain. Mea felt it in her soul—they hadn't lost them in Bristol at all. A greater demon had joined the hunt, masking their position and laying the foundation for a false sense of security.

"Can we make it to the car?" she asked.

Chris shook his head.

This was it then. The time they feared was upon them and they had to do whatever it took to protect the little girl in their charge. If tonight was the night they met their maker, then they wouldn't make it easy. Naturals did not kneel before Darkness, they fought to the last breath.

"Scarlett," she called, "come here."

The little girl discarded the blocks and ran into Mea's open arms, a grin plastered on her chubby face.

Picking her up, Mea hugged Scarlett tight, breathing in the lilac scent of the shampoo they used at bath time the night before.

"I need you to do something for me, sweetie. Something important. Do you think you can help me?"

The girl smiled and nodded, always eager to please. Scarlett was always such a well-behaved child. She hardly ever cried, had never thrown a tantrum, and had toilet trained herself. Mea remembered the day she found her in the bathroom of their latest flat, doing her business without being prompted. She was the envy of parents everywhere.

That's how Mea knew she didn't have to do much to get her into the metal box in the corner. Made from cold iron—metal extracted from a meteorite—it was the best last-minute protection they had.

She set the girl inside and made sure she was focused. "Scarlett, you have to hide, okay?"

Scarlett stared up at her with big eyes, her lip trembling. She could sense what was coming for them.

"It'll be okay, I promise," she said, glancing over her shoulder. "Stay very quiet, and I'll be back soon." She smoothed her hand through the girl's purple tresses and smiled. She was such a beautiful child and would break so many hearts when she became a woman. Mea had to make sure she made it that far. Once she manifested, then the Naturals—and the whole world—would have a chance at beating the Darkness.

"You're so brave, sweetie," she said, holding back tears.

Before Mea lost her nerve, she closed the lid of the box, sealing it with her Light. Hopefully, if anything happened to her and Chris, it'd mask Scarlett from the demons.

Standing, she joined Chris and unsheathed her arondight blade. Sparks flew across the tiny kitchen and their gazes met.

"I love you," he murmured. "If we die tonight, then we die well."

"For the Flame," she whispered as the door exploded inwards, "for Arondight."

I stood at one end of the training room deep within the London Sanctum, my gaze fixed on a paper target.

A cold iron dagger slammed into its mark, imbedding half an inch into the wood with deadly precision.

"Watch what I'm doing and not the target," Wilder said. "The only way you're going to hit what your aiming for is to perfect your throw."

He turned and demonstrated the correct stance, extending his arm. My gaze slid over his body, studying the lines of his muscled back instead of the way he held his arms, and I tensed. The second dagger collided into the target, imbedding right next to the first, and I blinked.

He turned, his eyes flashing silver in the light.

Ever since Wilder and I had joined our Light in the Necropolis, *things* had gotten worse. Inappropriate things to do with kissing and… Well, things that made my cheeks turn the same colour as my name.

My crush was literally crushing me every time we were in the same room. I supposed that's why people called them that. They never ended well because they never started to begin with.

What made it worse was that Wilder knew. We'd shared one kiss, but that was a long time ago and it'd never happened again. There'd been no discussion or acknowledgement, just the odd, thinly veiled manipulation when he wanted me to do something I didn't want to.

Everyone knew he had a thing for Greer. Perfect Greer, the head of the London Sanctum and protector of the Codex. She was powerful, beautiful, and in control—and the complete opposite of me.

Which is why I'd never stand a chance.

"*Scarlett.*"

I blinked, my gaze focusing on Wilder. "What?"

He frowned, but it turned out to be more of a scowl than anything. "Where the hell are you today?"

"In the pit of my despair," I drawled.

"Well, claw yourself out and focus. Training doesn't stop just because you killed one greater demon."

Markzoth, the Balan demon that murdered my parents and who'd spearheaded Human Convergence —the project designed to mutate innocent humans into demon super soldiers. Thinking about him made me wonder what my best friend, Jackson, was up to.

Jackson had fallen victim to the project, but

Ramona had been able to stop the mutation before it changed him completely. Now he was living with the Naturals in the Sanctum, helping us find a cure since there were others out there—lost, alone, and *changing*.

It was difficult not to take all of these things personally, especially since the entire world seemed hell-bent on capturing my purple arse. Markzoth, the demons, Julius Wainthrope. The ultimate prize was Arondight, and I had a part of it stuck inside me, turning my Light a funky neon purple.

I knew training was important, but there were some things I just couldn't let go of. Friends, family, truth…*love*.

I swallowed hard and turned my attention back to Wilder—my mentor, my teacher, my… Sometimes I didn't know what he was.

Wilder sighed sharply and held out a dagger towards me. "Throw it."

I snatched it and turned to the target. Lifting my left arm and holding my right—the one with the dagger—I balanced myself. Eyeing the target, I squared my jaw and threw.

The blade flew through the air, rotating hilt over tip, then slammed into the paper target with a dull thud. *Right between the eyes.*

Wilder grunted. He was waiting to scold me for not paying attention, but today I one-upped him.

"You've been practicing," he said.

"I can't rely on Arondight, can I?" I made a face and walked across the room to retrieve the daggers from the target.

"Don't get your pout on, Purples."

That was another after effect from the Necropolis. We'd begun to fight like cats and dogs, just like we had when we'd first met. Maybe it had something to do with how he'd called for back-up—using the secret booty call methods he shared with Greer—or maybe it was because I felt like I was being left behind. I could fight with at least ten different kinds of weapons —swords, daggers, staffs, and even several kinds of guns in the wake of Wainthrope's attempted coup— but I still hadn't mastered my Light.

"I can throw a bloody knife, Wilder," I exclaimed, wrenching out the first dagger. "What I can't do, is control the single most important thing about being a Natural."

"It's dangerous," he said, "you know that."

"Yeah, but it's who I am." I pull out the last two daggers and turned to face him. "You said it yourself —I'm just pretending to understand. Relying on dumb luck to survive won't work forever."

He narrowed his eyes.

"They've got to let me out sometime. Everyone's got a mission, even Jackson, and I'm here throwing cold iron daggers at targets photocopied onto A4 bits of paper sticky-taped together." I jabbed a finger at the latest one. "And the printer is out of toner!"

I looked away as the door opened, saving us from yet another argument.

"Oh, there you are," Romy declared. She was always happy-go-lucky, but her bright attitude rarely wore off on me, let alone Wilder. "Knife throwing.

My favourite!" She picked up a dagger and flipped it over in her hand. Wilder raised his eyebrow as she hurled the blade towards the target. When it slammed into the crotch area, she let out a whoop. "Bull's-eye!"

"Do I need to take out a restraining order?" Wilder asked.

Romy laughed and shook her head. "The council wants to see you both."

I bristled. I liked talking to Aldrich, but my growing jealousy of all things Greer-related was getting out of hand. That wasn't even mentioning Brax, who took surly to a whole new level.

"What do they want?" I asked. "Do you know?"

Romy shrugged. "I don't know. I just deliver the message."

"We're either in trouble or they want us to do something," Wilder declared.

I hadn't done anything *lately* so it must mean that they had an assignment for us, or they had some new information about my parents… or maybe it was a lead on Arondight.

"Her eyes are lighting up," Romy said to Wilder. "I know that look."

"Trouble," he drawled. "It always means trouble."

Two out of three council members were waiting for us in the library.

Most Naturals seemed allergic to books, but I liked

this place. It was quiet, smelt nice, and was a calm point in the brewing chaos of the world outside.

Our boots tapped on the hardwood floors as we walked the length of the room, passing the glass cases with their crazy artifacts—taxidermied butterflies and moths, various historically precious cold iron daggers, arrowheads and tools, Medieval jewellery, and other curiosities. Rows and rows of shelves of leather-bound books lined each wall, light spilling into each alcove from the windows on the left side.

At the end of the long corridor of books, the room opened up into a circular space. A domed skylight topped the space, where beyond, the sky was finally showing the first hints of springtime blue. Passing the columns, we stepped down into a seating area with crimson leather couches, armchairs, and matching carpet.

Greer was poised in one chair, while Aldrich lounged in another. He was a great deal more casual than the protector of the Codex, but today, his expression was serious.

"Where's Brax?" Wilder asked, narrowing his eyes.

"He's working with the Regula," Greer replied. "Hopefully, his presence can satisfy their concerns about how things are run here."

I squashed down the urge to scoff. The only way I could describe how leadership was running this place lately was 'reckless abandon'. No one seemed to know which way was true north anymore.

"Scarlett," her gaze found mine, "do you have something to say?"

"No."

Her stare was impassive and formal. "Please sit." She held out her hand, gesturing to the seats across from theirs.

I sat as far away from Greer as I could, and Wilder sat as close as he was able without raising suspicion. *Puke.*

"We've received intelligence that there may be a breach at the Academy," Greer stated, cutting to the chase. "There was an incident a few days ago that triggered the perimeter alarms, though an inspection of the grounds came up empty."

"That doesn't mean anything," Wilder said, his brow furrowing. "If something got through, there are plenty of places for it to hide."

"The faculty checked all the students," Aldrich explained. "None were possessed but as we know, Human Convergence is still in play, albeit in a small way. It doesn't take much to infect a host and the Academy is a target of interest for the demons."

I straightened up. "Are you saying you suspect one of the students has been infected with the same mutation as Jackson?"

"There have been signs that suggest something isn't right," Greer said with a nod. "The headmaster said there's a heaviness in the air that wasn't there before—an aggression that's not... *Natural.*"

"The Academy has always been cutthroat," Wilder said, looking bored. I got the feeling he wasn't interested in ever going back there, and I didn't blame him. But if something was wrong… "Besides, there are fail safes for this kind of thing."

"I've known Liam a long time," Greer stated. "I believe him, especially in these troubled times."

"Liam?" I asked.

"Liam Islington," Aldrich said. "He's the current headmaster of the Academy. He's a hard man, but a firm ally."

"Forgive me, but I've become skeptical of leadership lately," Wilder drawled. "We're not investigating the Academy because Islington has a *funny feeling*." He air quoted the last part, his eyes flashing silver.

"No, we're not," Greer said, her eyes narrowing in warning. "The council is ordering you because it's a valid threat."

"Both of us?" I looked at Wilder, whose scowl had deepened significantly.

"It's imperative you learn to control your Light," Greer said, jutting out her chin. "After the events at the Necropolis, it's clear you have an ability that can be both useful and dangerous. Attending the Academy will give you the opportunity to learn more about being a Natural." She turned to Wilder. "And you'll be the new combat instructor."

My breath caught. I wasn't sure if I was being handed exactly what I wanted or I'd just unwrapped the booby prize. They wanted me to go back to *high school?* It was traumatising enough the first time around, but this was the super elite Natural school of the bad-arse demon hunters.

And to state the glaringly obvious, I would be at least ten years older than everyone else. *Talk about humiliation central, population me.*

"Are you serious?" I asked, glancing between Greer and Aldrich. "You want me to enroll as a student?"

"You wanted out, Purples," Wilder drawled. "You've got your wish. I'm the one who's drawn the short straw."

"It's the perfect cover, Scarlett," Aldrich said. "You need to learn, and we need to make sure this threat is neutralised, if indeed there is a threat to begin with." *Two birds, one stone.*

"You've proved yourself to be a gifted instructor, Wilder," Greer said. "You'd be an asset to those students."

"When do we leave?" I didn't react well to snap decisions that sent me back to high school.

"Tomorrow morning," Aldrich said. "Everything has been arranged."

I groaned and slapped my hand against my forehead.

"It's not that bad," Greer said with a smile. "The instructor's are first rate. They're the best of the best."

"I know," I said, my shoulders sinking. "It's just… I wasn't the most popular kid at school the first time around."

"You'll be fine," Aldrich said, hiding a smile. "But

you'll have to keep your eyes and ears open. We can't let any of the students and staff know the underlying reason you're both there. If anyone's been compromised, the last thing we want is to tip them off."

"We're putting our trust in you," Greer added.

I hated that they were right. I was the perfect candidate to be a double agent. The embarrassment of being the first ever mature age student in Natural history was just an added benefit.

"Is that all?" Wilder asked, clearly annoyed with his newest assignment.

"Be ready to leave at oh-seven-hundred hours," Aldrich stated with a sharp nod.

Wilder stood and strode away, not even looking back at Greer. I smiled at them and followed him out of the library and into the hall.

Something was happening between Wilder and Greer and my jealous streak flared. He'd challenged her in front of me and Aldrich, and she'd cut him down brutally. His pride—and manhood—was obviously dented. Add a trip to the Academy into the mix, and I had an unstable nuclear reaction on my hands.

Knowing I'd be risking my life if I asked him about Greer, I went for the less explosive trigger. "I get the feeling you don't like this Islington guy," I said.

"I don't like anyone, Purples. You should know that by now." He was being evasive. *Typical.*

I blew through my lips and rolled my eyes. "As much as I love arguing with you, I will slap you down."

"I'd like to see you try."

I mulled over it for a moment. Wilder wasn't a fan of authority figures and his favourite pastime was flipping them the bird before doing whatever he wanted to get the job done. Until I came along, he barely followed any orders and was on the verge of being thrown out of the Sanctum entirely. I vaguely remembered someone telling me that his position here was tenuous at best, but Islington wasn't stationed here—he was at the Academy. People just didn't get appointed headmaster of educational institutions, which meant he'd been teaching there for a number of years prior.

Of course!

"You were at school together, weren't you?" I asked, the pieces clicking into place. "He was the school bu—"

"*Purples,*" he snapped.

"Well aren't we a pair of losers," I declared, flicking my purple hair over my shoulder. "I'm the twenty-five-year-old high school student, and you're the guy whose new boss was the kid who made your life a living hell."

Wilder growled and stalked off, causing me to run a few paces to catch up.

"If someone at that school is compromised, then we've got bigger problems, Purples," he stated. "They're going after kids now. They're the future of our species, if you want to get technical about it. If there aren't anymore Naturals being trained, then—"

"There'll be no one left to fight," I finished. The war was getting dirtier and dirtier.

"Greer and Aldrich are right. Someone has to go, and you need to learn. It's the perfect cover, and since I always seem to get lumped with you—"

"*Arsehole.*" I flipped him the bird and spun on my heel. Stalking down the hall, I swallowed my anger. Just when I thought we were getting closer.

"Where are you going?" he called after me.

"If we're leaving tomorrow, then I want to say bye to Jackson."

"*Scarlett…*"

I glanced over my shoulder as I rounded the corner, catching one last glimpse of my mentor. His hands were shoved into his pockets and he looked almost sheepish. *Good.*

I knocked on Jackson's door, punctuating the rap with my forehead.

His voice echoed from inside. "*Yeah?*"

I pushed inside and slammed the door behind me. My best friend was lying on the bed with a PlayStation controller in his hand. I couldn't believe they let him bring his console and gave him an internet connection to go with it. It was encrypted up the wazoo, but that wasn't the point. I wasn't even allowed to have a mobile phone.

"I know that look," he said.

"What look?"

Jackson had always been this lanky, nerdy guy but after his mutation, he'd grown into his body and then some. He had muscles on top of muscles, enhanced strength and hearing, and had ditched his glasses for good. The six-foot bean pole was looking more like an underwear model than the professional gamer he was six months ago.

He made a face. "Are you and Wilder still fighting?"

"What do you think?" I pouted and flopped down on the bed next to him.

He was playing an open-world RPG. Some post-apocalyptic thing. I hoped it wasn't an omen, or a glimpse into humanity's imminent future if Light failed.

"Have you told him about your fe—"

"*No.*"

My cheeks flushed and I stared at the paused screen on the TV. How did I tell Wilder that joining my Arondight sliced Light to his ordinary Natural Light, had only fanned the flames of the unobtainable lust I had for him? *I didn't*, that's how. The only logical thing to do was pick fight after fight and let my jealousy percolate.

"If you told him—"

"No," I snapped, "I can't tell him anything."

"He already suspects," Jackson stated. "You know he does. Besides, *he* kissed you."

"Like six months ago." I rolled my eyes. "The window for following that up has well and truly closed."

He clucked his tongue and shook his head, clearly disapproving. "You know how I feel about it, Scarlett. I'm not going to keep hitting you over the head with it."

"Maybe going back to school will be a good thing, then," I mused. Learning from new teachers in a new environment. No more close quarters with Wilder would hopefully cool things down before they *embarrassingly* exploded in my face.

"Wait," Jackson tilted his head to the side, "what?"

"I'm leaving on a mission tomorrow," I said. "Well, I'm not sure it's a mission or one of those crazy do-overs like *Freaky Friday* or that Drew Barrymore movie, *Never Been Kissed*."

"What are you on about?"

"I'm going to the Academy. *To learn.*"

Jackson snorted, then started to laugh. "You're going back to high school?"

"Demon hunter high school," I corrected. "It's like Hogwarts, but a thousand times more deadly. *They give the kids knives.*"

"You wanted to learn how to use your Light," he reasoned. "Now you've got a chance to learn from a *certified* teacher."

"And one who's not scared I'm going to melt him from the inside out." I sighed, my chest rising and falling.

"Can you really blame him?" He patted me on the shoulder. "After what you told me about blowing up that tosser, Markzoth…" Not to mention everything else I'd done—facing the druidess and her overpowered runes, healing Jackson's mortal wounds, and practically syphoning the Light out of my mentor. "I wonder if he just doesn't know how to help you. Like, a pride thing. He seems the type of guy who hates losing."

I grunted and picked up the controller. "What game are you playing?"

"Don't change the subject."

"Party pooper."

"I love you, Scarlett, but you're infuriating when you're on the heartbreak spiral."

He was right, which made me feel even worse. I was such a Negative Nancy lately. "Careful, or I won't send you any owls when I'm away at school."

Jackson smirked and took the controller out of my hands. "This sounds like a good thing. You need to learn how to control the piece of Arondight inside you, and…" he trailed off. "There's something else happening, isn't there?"

"Yeah, but I'm not sure I'm supposed to say."

"That's cool." He shrugged. "I know you guys have to go out and do your super secret spy thing, but just be careful, okay?"

"Always." Except the times I was recklessly running headfirst into danger. Which was pretty much at every opportunity.

"Hey." He picked up a strand of my hair and twisted it around his fingers. "Is your hair more purple, or is it just me?"

Plucking my hair out of his grasp, I squinted at the flecks of violet. "Na, it's just the light in here."

Jackson shrugged and said, "Anyway, since you're going away…" he wrapped his arm around my shoulders and squeezed, "wanna hang out for a while?"

"Sure," I smiled, watching the screen as he unpaused the game, "I'd love to."

2

———

The Cotswolds were a two-hour drive directly west of London.

Nestled between Oxford and Glouster, the landscape was full of rolling hills, grassland, forests, quaint little Medieval villages, and stately homes. There were even ruined castles and ancient Roman amphitheaters and forts amongst the wilderness. It was nice to be out of the city—the heaviness of the urban sprawl was even more depressing now that I knew what was lurking within it.

I sat in the front passenger seat of a black sedan, my bag stashed in the back seat. Wilder was behind the wheel, taking the corners on the narrow country road a little too fast for my liking.

The coin the druidess gave me weighed heavily in my pocket, and I ran my thumb over the surface. I hadn't told anyone about it, not even Wilder. That night was a burden on my mind, knowing she'd been waiting for me to return. The coin was something that related to my past, but it was also a symbol of the extinction of the Druids. Jackson argued that it was self-defence, but it didn't feel like it to me.

I couldn't tell Wilder that the sweet—yet frustratingly selfish—woman who he'd brought seeds and chocolate bars to was dead. Though, I wondered if he already knew. Wilder always knew when something was up, which made my unrequited crush even more embarrassing than it needed to be.

I ran my fingers over the rough surface of the coin again. I'd hardly looked at it, yet I carried it everywhere I went. "Do they have a library here?"

"It's a school," Wilder replied, "of course they do."

The car rounded a corner and the trees parted, giving us a breathtaking view of the patchwork landscape. In the distance, I caught a glimpse of a manor house and gardens. It was a big grey building with tall windows and turrets—a mix between the red brick Tudor and dreary Victorian styles of architecture.

"Is that the Academy?" I asked, plastering my nose against the window.

"Some of it," Wilder replied.

"Some?"

"It's protected by powerful cloaking and illusions," he explained. "Only a small section is visible to maintain appearances with the locals."

"How big is it?" Staring at the grounds from this distance, it was difficult to tell where the illusions began.

"About five times what you see."

"Five times?" My mouth fell open.

"Don't worry, Purples, you'll see it up close soon enough." He swerved around a bend in the road, narrowly missing a car coming the other way. The left-hand mirror sideswiped the hedge and I snapped my head away from the window.

"Seeing you drive is weird," I said as my heartbeat returned to normal. "I didn't know you had your licence."

"I don't," he replied, turning off the road and onto a gravel driveway.

I tensed as we drove through a large pair of wrought-iron gates, glad we'd arrived in one piece.

The illusion hanging around the grounds shimmered as we drove through it, revealing a house much larger than I'd seen from the road. It was just like Wilder said—the Academy was massive.

The manor house stretched into several wings, the central portion of the complex surrounded a courtyard, and outside the main entrance was a large fountain with a marble statue of none other than the Lady of the Lake. The rest of the grounds were hidden by the imposing grey structure, but I knew there were acres of gardens, sports fields, grassland, and woods that all belonged to the Naturals.

"*Great*," Wilder drawled.

Looking up, I noticed there were several figures standing outside the main building, obviously waiting for us.

"Who are they?" I asked, craning my neck.

"Faculty." He didn't seem to be in a talkative mood, which had been the tone he'd set the moment we'd left the Sanctum.

"How much do they know exactly?"

"The bare minimum."

"So don't go around talking about Human Convergence, then?"

"No."

Wilder pulled up beside the welcoming party and killed the engine. He gave me a pointed look that warned me not to let my tongue loose before he got out of the car.

We had our briefing at the Sanctum. I knew we had to keep quiet about the mutations, but it didn't make it any easier. It was like I was the new agent at MI6, and this was a clandestine operation into arms dealing or something equally diabolical. But I supposed it was in a way.

Climbing out of the passenger seat, I rounded the bonnet of the car and joined Wilder and the people waiting for us.

The first was an authoritative-looking man who looked as if he was trying to pull off the hip, relaxed teacher vibe. He wore back jeans, boots, a light blue business shirt with an unbuttoned collar, and a navy suit jacket. His hair was precision cut and combed into place with a sharp side part, and his jaw was clean shaven. Looking him over, I wondered who he was. His jacket even had leather patches over the elbows.

The woman next to him was dishevelled in

comparison. Her curly chestnut-coloured hair was dragged up into a messy topknot, her glasses had a smudge across the right lens, and she was dressed in an assortment of colours and patterns. Her black corduroy pencil skirt reached her knees and underneath, she had on a pair of black- and purple-striped tights. She had that whole art teacher vibe going on.

Both didn't look a day over thirty or thirty-five, though I wasn't a good judge of age. The way Wilder was glaring at the man was an indicator that he must be the dreaded headmaster.

"You must be Miss Ravenwood," the man said. "Welcome to the Academy. I'm Liam Islington, the headmaster." *Bingo*. He thrust his hand towards me, and I was forced to take it in my own. Shaking, I glanced at the woman next to him. "This is Adelaide Hawthorne, Director of Student Affairs."

"Oh, don't be so formal, Liam," she said smiling at me. "I'm the guidance councillor."

Wilder snorted, drawing Islington's attention.

"Mr. Wilder," he said, gazing at him coolly. "When Greer said you'd be the operative accompanying Miss Ravenwood, I was surprised you agreed to the assignment."

Wilder leaned forwards, towering over Islington. "What's so surprising about it? If I remember correctly, I was best in our class."

"You had a rebellious streak and a disdain for authority that I can see still exists. I don't want that rubbing off on the students," he replied. "You're here to teach them combat. I expect you to leave the lessons in analytical thinking to their Ethics classes."

Burn. It was my turn to snort. I was beginning to see why they'd been rivals at school. The two men were polar opposites in the worst possible way—*the stabby kind*.

"This place is massive. Is there time to see the grounds before we go inside?" I asked, attempting to defuse the tension. "Or am I required to start classes straight away?"

"Of course," the headmaster replied. "I can take you part of the way and Adelaide can assist with settling you into your accommodations. Official classes began a month ago, but you will both begin tomorrow."

"Thanks." I nodded as Islington gestured for us to follow him around the side of the main house. I glanced over my shoulder at the fountain in the driveway—the Lady of the Lake's stone eyes seemed to follow our path.

Our boots crunched on the cream-coloured gravel as we passed under several large windows. Inside, I could see a handful of students milling about and my curiosity tingled.

"It's a rare honour for the faculty to teach the only living Natural who's touched Arondight," Islington said.

Tensing, I glanced at Adelaide, who wasn't even looking at me. "Do the other students know who I am?"

"They do," Islington replied. "Rumours are difficult to stop once they gain momentum."

Great. Either I'd fit right in, or I'd be subjected to a slew of hazing rituals.

"You'll be head cheerleader before you know it, Purples," Wilder quipped.

I elbowed him in the gut. "*Unlikely.*"

Moving around the corner, we stepped down a flight of stone stairs and found ourselves in a traditional English garden. Impeccably manicured box hedges lined the path, and raised garden beds housed various rose bushes and cottage flowers— white daisies, purple lavender, a rainbow of hollyhock, and violet asters.

"The Naturals have held this land for almost eight hundred years," the headmaster explained as we walked past a marble statue of a naked lady with a sword. "The borders are well-established, along with security systems—modern and Light-infused."

"But something still got through," Wilder declared.

I shot him a warning glare. "No security system is infallible when something wants to get through bad enough."

"The alarms were triggered, so they didn't fail," Adelaide declared.

Wilder grunted but didn't press. His gaze was flicking everywhere, taking in the Academy he'd spent so much of his youth at. I remembered he'd told me he'd remained here during term breaks because he had no family to visit. Christmas, Easter, and summer holidays were all spent in the confines of this place. I wondered if he considered it home, or if he remembered it the same way I did all those foster homes I passed through.

"We appreciate your presence, Wilder," Islington drawled, "but we don't want to alarm the students. There has been no reason to suggest anyone has been possessed, so this is merely a precaution. If something is testing our defences, then we'd prefer to be prepared if there is a next time."

"And the added benefits, of course," Adelaide said, making moon eyes at Wilder. She obviously found him attractive, and who could blame her? Not me. "The students will cherish the opportunity to learn from an active Natural." She turned her smile to me. "And you can learn more about your heritage, Scarlett."

"How many students study here?" I asked her.

"About a hundred."

"Only a hundred?" Shocked, I looked up at the building, the two-story wing towering above us.

"We're a dwindling race, Miss Ravenwood," Islington remarked. "This is the lowest number of students we've ever had. These are dire times, so you can understand why we made the request to the London Sanctum."

It seemed like such a shame. Demons were only increasing in numbers and the Naturals were dying out, not because of the war but because of basic biology. I was starting to see why our appointment here was so non-negotiable.

"On the left, you can see the wing of the Academy which houses most of our classrooms," Islington said, holding his hand towards the façade of the building. "Students are required to take several theory programs. They are demonology, history, ethics, math, biology, and science."

"Science?" I asked, my brow creasing.

"We live in an ever-evolving world, Miss Ravenwood. Technology is always encroaching into our lives, effecting the balance between Light and Dark."

"It's not only technology, but biological science," Wilder said. "Understanding how our enemy works is extremely important in learning how we could one day defeat them."

"Of course," I said with a smile. Human Convergence was the thing on everyone's mind at the London Sanctum, and the underlying reason we were here.

"There are a number of corresponding practical classes," Islington said, continuing his overview. "Light studies and combat training. Both are broken down into various sub-courses, but they take up much of the curriculum. We are training warriors here, and we need to arm them with as much knowledge—mental *and* physical—as we are able." He checked his watch, then turned to me. "I understand you've already been granted your arondight blade."

I nodded. "I have."

"Typically, students aren't given their blades until

they graduate, so I must request that you surrender yours until your training has been completed."

A heavy feeling settled in my gut and I was overly conscious of the weight of the hilt in my jacket pocket. Separating a Natural from their arondight blade? *Nah ah.*

"It will be placed in the vault," he explained. "No one will be able to touch it, Miss Ravenwood. It will be perfectly safe there."

"You're a student now, Purples," Wilder said. "Showing favouritism would draw unwanted attention. We don't want to alarm any of the students."

"He's right," Adelaide said with a kind smile. "They have enough pressure without knowing their safety may be at risk."

Swallowing hard, I reluctantly took out my arondight blade. Holding it in my hand, I memorised the feel of it—the weight and design—before handing it to the headmaster. At least he didn't ask for the cold iron dagger hidden in my boot.

"Take care of it?"

"Of course." He slipped the hilt into the inside pocket of his jacket. "If you'll excuse me, I have business to attend to." He glared at Wilder. "If you'd like to come with me, we have a few matters to discuss your position."

Adelaide and I watched the two men walk away. Standing awkwardly, I glanced at her.

"He's very… *proper.*"

"Liam's okay," she said, looking after their

receding forms. Her head tilted slightly to the side and I knew she was checking out Wilder's arse.

I coughed, drawing her attention back to me. "Where to now?"

"Let's get you oriented with the grounds."

I shrugged, glad to be led for once.

"It must be strange returning to school after so long," she said, leading me through a side door.

"I've got a good ten years on the senior class," I retorted. "What do you think?"

"This isn't a traditional school, Scarlett. You're welcome here."

I narrowed my eyes, but didn't argue with her. Kids were right about adults being out of touch, but I found myself wondering at what point that happened. Was it a switch that flipped one day? Was it a certain experience or age that determined the shift? I didn't know, but what I did understand was that kids stuck together in their cliques like pack animals, and I was *one of them*.

Adelaide treated me to the extended grand tour of the Academy. After we'd wandered through the halls and peered into classrooms, we ventured through the kitchens for some lunch, then strolled by the gym and training rooms where students were being drilled in various combat techniques.

Kids of all ages were represented—from ten to seventeen—and it was a strange sight seeing a bunch of primary-aged students fighting with staffs. They were so well behaved.

Outside, Adelaide showed me the soccer pitch, the

tennis courts, and the indoor swimming pool. Once my eyes had been shoved back into my head, she pointed out the boundary of the grounds. The first was where the students were allowed to roam, and the second was the ultimate border of the property.

By the time we returned to the manor for the dormitory tour, the sun had already begun to set.

Like the other wings, it was two-story and separated right down the middle by shared common rooms. One side was for the boys, the other for the girls. Upstairs were the senior classes and the younger kids were downstairs. The faculty apartments were in a wing deeper in the complex.

"And here is your room." Adelaide opened the door at the end of the hall, revealing a shoebox. It wasn't unlike any London flats if you asked me.

A single bed with a simple wooden frame was pushed up against the left wall, a desk and a closet was against the right. A window with a box seat was at the end, bookending the door we'd just walked in. There was only just enough room for both of us to stand in the remaining floor space.

My bag had made it up here somehow and sat on the foot of the bed.

"This is… cozy," I declared.

"It isn't much, but there's a common room at the end of the hall with couches, games, books, and a TV. Breakfast is at six, and classes begin at eight." She thrust a piece of crumpled paper at me. "Here's your schedule."

I plucked the timetable from her hand and peered

at it. The first class in the morning was Light Studies. "Diving in headfirst, I see."

"The best time to start is now," she declared, handing me a key which I guessed was to my room. "Come with me. I want to introduce you to one of our brightest students."

I followed her out into the hall, our footsteps muffled on the carpet runner. Every inch of space in this place was either adorned with elaborate draperies, old-timey paintings, sculptures, or Medieval-style weapon displays—just like a historic English manor house was supposed to.

Adelaide rapped her knuckles against a door four down from mine.

It was wrenched open, revealing an angsty teenage girl. I immediately got the sense she was the alternative goth type, A.K.A. the outsider. The exact kid I was when I was seventeen—dyed black hair, sharp fringe, smeared smoky eyeliner, ivory skin, and stompy combat boots. She looked cool to me, but I knew the other kids probably saw her as too weird to fit into their moulds.

"Ah, Madeleine," Adelaide said, ignoring the girl's cold stare, "this is our new student, Scarlett."

She looked at me. "She's old."

"I'm twenty-five," I stated. "It's not *old*. Besides, thirty is the new twenty." Thankfully this wasn't the kind of school that required uniforms, otherwise it would be even more humiliating.

The girl rolled her eyes, clearly not impressed. "Whatever."

"Scarlett is starting classes tomorrow," Adelaide went on, oblivious to the silent challenge happening between me and Madeleine. "Could you buddy up with her? Show her to the kitchens and her first class?"

The girl spun a strand of black hair around her finger and looked me over. "Cool hair," she said after a moment.

"Thanks. Purple's my thing."

"Yeah. I know." She sighed heavily and pouted. "Breakfast's at six. I won't wait for you." The door slammed in our faces and I blinked.

"Well, that was welcoming," I drawled, scratching my head.

Adelaide smiled brightly and patted me on the shoulder. "See? What did I tell you?"

3

The next morning Madeleine walked me to breakfast… and promptly dumped me at the door.

I couldn't blame her, really. Unwanted attention wasn't high on her priority list and besides, I was a grown-up who could walk herself to class.

I ate on my own, enduring the curious stares from the other students. No one was brave enough, or interested enough, to approach me, and I felt a pang in my heart. Nothing had changed. The way I remembered life at school was exactly the same, even if the Naturals thought they were different from humans. We all had the same faults and attributes. Sticking to the familiar, forming packs, putting weight behind things that didn't matter in the real world— popularity, beauty, power. Scratch that. Those things still totally ruled grown-up's lives, they were just levelled up.

I found my way to Light Studies without much

fuss. The hallways were busy with students rushing back and forth, shouting, laughing, and jostling one another. It was a refreshing change from the dour mood at the Sanctum, and I was already starting to forget that outside the grounds, a war was being fought.

I found a seat in the middle of the cluster of desks and set my notebook and pen down in front of me. The classroom was once part of a series of private rooms, called an apartment that stretched the length of the entire wing. I wasn't sure which this used to be —the parlour or the dressing room—but the walls were lined with a mint green wallpaper, gilded filagree, and wood panelling. The ceiling was painted with a Renaissance-era fresco with a Natural twist— armour-clad knights, delicate ladies in waiting, kings, and princesses, and the Lady of the Lake in her flowing robes and impossibly long hair.

At the front of the room was a larger desk and a blackboard on wheels, and behind that were three sets of gigantic panelled bay windows that ran almost to the ceiling. Within each nook were bench seats lined with emerald-coloured velvet. Outside, I caught a glimpse of the Academy grounds and the rolling Cotswold landscape beyond.

It took me a while, but I gradually became aware of a looming presence. Dark, angry, and doing their best to exert their power of influence. I looked up and wasn't surprised at what I found. Three menacing girls glared at me and I stared back, waiting for the other shoe to drop.

The one in the centre was obviously the leader. They all had the physique of a Natural—lean, yet muscular—but she was tall, blonde, had flawless skin, and was the kind of girl who walked the halls and had rose petals thrown before her. The others had darker colouring, but were no less pretty. They were Brittany's back-up singers.

"I'm Kayla," the blonde girl said, ruining my punch line. "And this is Trish and Maisy."

I stared up at them and a chill ran down my spine. It was like I was staring at a cliché. "Okay?"

Kayla rolled her eyes. "And you're in my seat."

"I didn't know these seats were assigned."

"*They aren't.*"

Her challenge was clear. She ruled the Academy and wanted to make sure everyone knew it, even me.

They glared at me, waiting. They wanted me to move, and the stubborn streak in me was daring me to stay put. Remembering my mission, and Greer's disproving stare when Islington calls her about my inevitable day-one detention, I caved.

Sighing, I picked up my notebook and pen, and rose to my feet. I was twenty-five, I should be immune to this shite.

Flipping my hair, I walked away, finding another seat at the back of the class.

The boy next to me gave me a look, then leaned towards me. "Hey, I'm Trent." He punctuated the announcement with a cocky smile that had flirt written all over it.

He was a handsome guy with his sandy blond hair,

chiselled jaw, and teenage muscles, but he had a baby face and was under legal age.

"I'm pretty sure you're jail bait," I hissed.

"Maybe in the human world," he replied, turning up the charm. "But you're in our world now. Age is nothing when you have this…" He held up his hand and a spark of Light began to form in his palm. White tendrils grew, twisting around each other, growing larger until his creation was complete—a shimmering white rose bud.

Ugh, puke.

The door burst open and a man strode in, his trajectory lining up with the desk at the front of the room. Middle-aged, salt and pepper hair, tough guy exterior. A typical teacher type with magical powers, then.

Trent closed his hand, absorbing the rose, and sat back in his seat. I felt the burning dagger of a teenage girl's jealousy stab me in the face, and I glanced up. Kayla was looking at me over her shoulder, disapproval clear in her features. She obviously liked Trent, or at least had a claim over him, but Trent was a loose cannon *if you know what I mean.*

"Good morning, everyone," the teacher said, dumping his bag onto the desk. "For the first time in the history of the Academy, we have a new student in the senior class."

Senior class? I glanced around the room as everyone turned to stare at me. I was in the senior Light class? That couldn't be right. I mean, I didn't know *anything…*

You did kill Markzoth, I thought. *You've gotta know something.* But was that me or Arondight?

"Scarlett Ravenwood." The teacher craned his neck, looking for me. I wasn't hard to miss. "I'm Mr. Masters. Would you care to stand up and introduce yourself?"

I groaned and clicked my pen a dozen times as fast as I could. Why did teachers always want the new kids to give their life stories on their first day? As if turning up at a fresh school as the new and shiny weirdo wasn't bad enough, they had to put me on exhibition, too.

How many times had I done it? Five or six, *at least.* After the first two, I made up a different story every time, just to make things difficult. It hardly mattered because I knew I'd either get expelled or moved to another foster home before the year was out. But I was grown now, and I'd faced worse than a bunch of hormone-enraged teenagers.

I stood, my gaze scanning the students. There were about a dozen or so in the class, all of them sitting in their friendship groups. The mean girls, Kayla, Maisy, and Trisha, a group of boys that looked like the jocks, a bunch of regular kids—the kind that sat in the middle of the hierarchy—and a new breed of teenager was amongst them… the hardcore Natural. For them, training was serious business—they'd grow up to be the career soldiers like Romy, Alo, and the others. They'd walk the beat until the day they died.

Blinking, I took a deep breath. "I'm Scarlett. I'm

from London. I've been training at the Sanctum there after I found out I was a Natural last winter."

"She's practically a geriatric," Kayla whispered loudly enough so everyone could hear.

"*Kayla*," Mr. Masters snapped, "please leave your childish arrogance at the door. We're training you to become a Natural, not a gossip columnist." The class sniggered.

"Yeah, I'm older than everyone else, so what?" I turned my gaze onto the mean girls. "I wasn't as lucky as you are to have your whole life to dedicate to becoming a Natural. So I was transferred here so I can learn, and that's what I intend to do." I sat down, suddenly aware that my heart was thumping in my chest. Was I having a panic attack? I knew school was tough, but I need get a grip!

Trent gave me a double thumbs up and I sank back into my seat with a groan.

"All right, all right," Mr. Masters said, waving his hand at us. "Now, let's pick up where we left off. Levitation. Miss Ravenwood? Would you care to come to the front and show me where your level is at?"

"I don't think…" I glanced warily at the other students. "I, uh—"

"Your existence is hardly a secret, Miss Ravenwood, or is it that you think your status warrants special treatment?"

Kayla smirked triumphantly at me and I wrinkled my nose. My funky Light didn't warrant being singled out, but Mr. Masters seemed to think it made me a prime candidate for demonstration. They'd see it soon enough, so I may as well get it out of the way.

I made my way confidently to the front of the class, where Masters piled up a series of hardcover books. I hadn't levitated anything before, but how hard could it be? Wilder had taught me about intent, so if I didn't overdo it, then this should be easy as pie.

I looked at Masters, waiting for his instructions.

"Levitate the books, Miss Ravenwood." That's all he gave me.

Okay then… I took a deep breath and held out my hand. My fingertips sparked purple and the class leaned forward, suddenly interested. They began to murmur so much, Masters snapped at them to be quiet.

"Close out all other sounds," he said. "Focus on bringing your Light forward, then your intent."

I felt the same spark that Wilder had coaxed out of me back at his safe house and the rush of power I'd felt at the Necropolis. They were one and the same, and before I realised what I was doing, a burst of Light flared out of my hand and Mr. Masters was flying across the classroom.

I slapped my hand over my mouth in shock as he managed to stop himself just short of slamming into the wall. He hovered there for a moment as the class burst out into fits of riotous laughter, then his feet touched the ground.

"That's enough!" he bellowed. Then he turned his glare onto me. *"Miss Ravenwood."*

I grimaced and offered him a confused shrug. "Sorry?"

"Clearly, we have more work to do with you than we first anticipated."

"I'll say," Kayla quipped, causing the other students to snigger.

***

The Academy kitchen was just like the one at the Sanctum.

Long tables ran the length of the room, a mix of bench seats and chairs along either side, and at one end was a large buffet-style spread with a choice of hot and cold foods. Naturally, all of them were healthy options. There were no chicken nuggets or French fries in sight, but I'd already acclimatised to the sugar-free diet Wilder had assigned me when we'd first started training together.

I chose a garden salad with a side of grilled chicken and found an empty spot at the far end of the hall. What better place to observe teenagers in their natural pecking order than during feeding time at the zoo?

The cliques were all the stereotypical types, spread out over the four different class years. Junior, intermediate, advanced, and senior. There were the popular girls, the tough guys, the nerds, the outcasts, the trouble makers, that one guy all the girls had a crush on, and finally, the one who ruled them all. *Kayla.*

Rolling my eyes, I wondered if she was the one harbouring a little Human Convergence. Wouldn't that be poetic?

Staring at my schedule, I realised my afternoon theory classes—demonology and history—were all with the junior and intermediates. Talk about a demotion. Thankfully, combat training was a solo affair with a new instructor. Wilder wouldn't be teaching me at all and I wasn't sure if I was happy about it.

Laughter drew my attention to a group of kids sitting a few spaces down from me. Looking at me, they whispered at each other before giggling again. They looked like they were all barely scraping up against puberty—twelve or thirteen, if I was going to guess.

"What?" I demanded, putting on my scary adult face.

"I, uh… We heard that your Light is purple," the closest boy said.

"Is that true?" the girl next to him asked.

I narrowed my eyes and studied each of them. "Yes."

"I knew it," the boy hissed to the others.

"Why are you here?" the girl asked, becoming bolder. "You're kind of old to be at school."

"I only found out I was a Natural six months ago," I replied, stabbing a slice of tomato with my fork. "I didn't get the same education as everyone else."

The boy pouted. "How could you not know?"

"My parents died when I was barely out of nappies." I shrugged. "I fell into the foster system and all the stories you hear are true." I made a face and went back to my salad.

"Is it true you were at the London Sanctum?" the boy asked.

I nodded.

"Have you seen the Codex?" the girl chimed in.

The boy's eyes widened. "What's it like?"

"It's like a book." A mystical, magical book—full of the complete history of the Naturals since the cataclysm—that cooked the unworthy from the inside out. The kids stared at me, unable to hide their disappointment. "It's hard to explain," I added. "It's full of Light, and not like the copies they give us. There are hand-drawn illuminations, pages written by all the people you hear about in class, and it's like… Well, it's like it has its own mind. It knows things."

"That's what my sister said," the girl stated. "She saw it once, you know." She puffed out her chest proudly, her one degree of separation obviously meaning the world to her.

The students nodded enthusiastically and began to murmur amongst themselves.

Returning to my lunchtime snooping, I scanned the hall. The mean girls—Kayla, Trisha, and Maisy— were sitting on the opposite table, a few seats down. They were laughing and whispering, flashing flirty looks at the boys. Each wore the Natural uniform of black T-shirt and tactical trousers, which I gathered meant they were in for an afternoon of fight training.

"Have you seen the new combat instructor?" Maisy asked.

"Yes," Kayla gushed. "He's so *hot.*"

"Trent said he's from the London Sanctum."

"He was top of his class, apparently," Kayla said matter-of-factly. "I can't wait to learn from him."

Trisha snorted and fanned herself. "Yeah right, *learn.*"

Kayla flipped her hair behind her shoulder. "He can spar with me *anytime.*"

"What's his name?" Trisha asked.

Maisy fluttered her eyebrows. "*Wilder.*"

"*Wild...*" Kayla winked suggestively, and the group burst out into fits of giggles.

Swallowing a pile of vomit, I turned back to the rest of my chicken. I didn't know how long we were going to be here, but I knew it was going to be a *riot.*

Thankfully the rest of the day went smoother, but the story of the new girl throwing a senior teacher across a classroom had spread far and wide.

Just wait until Wilder hears about it. I was already anticipating the relentless teasing.

Walking down the hall, I scanned my schedule, wondering when I had combat training. I was much better at fighting than taking notes.

"Hey, *geriatric.*"

I glanced up as the mean girl trio stalked past and rolled my eyes. *Pfft, whatever.*

My first day had been so hectic, I'd hardly had any time to keep an eye on the other students, and mine and Wilder's mission was already becoming muddy. Hopefully, he'd had a better start, though I was glad to have some time apart. Maybe I'd become too reliant on him always being around. Clear head, clear heart and all.

Spotting Madeleine further down the hall, I started walking towards her. If anyone could give me the run down of who was who in this place, it was her. If I knew the status quo, spotting anomalies in behaviour would be easier.

Kayla slammed her shoulder into Madeleine's and the goth girl's books went flying. Papers skidded across the hall and laughter rang out as the mean girl trio walked away, whispering and glancing back at their victim.

My lips thinned in disapproval. *Kids still did this petty shite to one another?*

Madeleine bent over to pick up her books, her hair falling forward to create a dark curtain covering her heated cheeks. Other students merely stepped over her, no one lingered to help.

In that moment, I saw a lot of myself in her—the outcast, never fitting in anywhere. Too different to belong with the alternative kids. An easy target. Society's stereotypical punching bag.

"Here, let me help," I said, kneeling beside her. Scooping up the papers that'd fallen out of her folder, I held them out.

She eyed me warily, then tentatively plucked the notes from my hand. "Thanks."

I smiled and held out my hand. "I'm Scarlett, remember? You dumped me at breakfast?"

"I know who you are," she said, glancing at my hand. She didn't make a move to take it and I pulled back awkwardly.

"Good. I was beginning to think I was forgettable."

"How? You blew Mr. Masters across the classroom this morning."

I snorted and covered my mouth with my hand to stop myself from laughing. Well, it was funny.

"That was an accident. He shouldn't have stood in the line of fire." I rose to my feet and dusted off my jeans.

"He wasn't in the line of fire."

The only way she could have known that was if she was there, but I didn't remember seeing her. Was she that good at making herself small?

"I didn't know you were in that class," I said.

She stood and slid her books into her backpack. "No one knows I'm in any class."

I frowned, knowing exactly why she did it. She didn't want to make herself a target, Self-preservation, a strategy I was all too familiar with.

"It gets better, you know," I said.

She lowered her gaze and I knew she was fighting back tears. "Everyone says that."

"That's because it's true."

"It doesn't help me now, does it?" Her sadness

turned to anger and she glared at me before stalking off.

Turning, I watched her disappear. Madeleine was right. What happened now, would shape how she saw the world when she finally went out into it. I thought about Wilder and his surly attitude. *Case in point.*

But for a Natural whose sole job was to be a soldier of Light fighting the demon horde? I wasn't sure it was a good thing.

4

The ceiling of my bedroom wasn't that interesting. I lay on my bed, my mind utter chaos.

Outside, the sun was setting, the last rays of orange light filtered through the old wibbly wobbly glass panels in the window. Holding the coin in the air, I turned it over and over, studying the markings.

The silver disc wasn't large, maybe an inch in diameter with the thickness of a pound coin. One side had a sword in the centre, which I believed to be a representation of Arondight, and two symbols on either side, making four in total. On the other side was a crude impression of a flame and writing that snaked around the outside, following the curve of the coin. It was all worn, the metal somehow softened from being handled, and the words were almost illegible. What I could make out sounded like Latin, but without internet access, I couldn't consult Google Translate.

The only place left where I could find answers was the library.

Sighing, I rolled off the bed and went out into the hall. Moving into the common room, I found it empty. It obviously wasn't the popular place to be at seven on a Friday night. Wherever the other teenagers hung out, I wasn't invited... *yet.*

Determined not to be the person who moped in her shoebox bedroom, I wandered out of the dormitory and walked the length of the Academy. Moving into the parts I hadn't seen yet, I finally came across the place I was looking for.

I hadn't been shown the library on the tour Adelaide had given me, along with a lot of other hidden nooks and crannies I'd passed on the way here. With curiosity winning out, I pushed through the door.

I wasn't expecting it to be so large—it dwarfed the space at the Sanctum. Sturdy bookshelves lined every available wall, and rows jutted out, each capped with brass plates and reference numbers. A bank of old-fashioned drawers housed a card catalogue towards one side—something I hadn't seen since childhood. Caramel-coloured tables with green padded tops and green and gold lamps were clustered to the left, and a staircase led up to a second floor, where more bookcases stretched into infinity and beyond.

It smelt like a secondhand bookstore in here, mixed with the odd scent of furniture polish and peppermint. A chair creaked somewhere, someone coughed, and a book snapped shut. Glancing around,

I noticed a few groups of students huddled over books and laptops, working on assignments. It was otherwise empty.

I wandered farther into the cavernous room, studying the glass display cases. They were full of rare books, Natural artifacts, weapons, arrowheads, jewellery, assorted coins, and magical relics that looked a lot like the runes Wilder and I had retrieved for the druidess.

The shadows here were long, and the silence too obvious for my liking. Magic and mystery were housed here, but it was hardly surprising considering where I was.

I stopped at the foot of the stairs, my gaze caught on an incredible sight. A full suit of armour with a sword in hand was displayed in the centre of the action, the warm lights shining off the metal.

I walked around the glass case that housed it, studying each intricate piece—coif, pauldron, greaves, and gauntlets. I didn't know the names of other parts, but I had Jackson to thank for what little knowledge I did have. Some games he liked to play had complicated armour systems, though the armour in front of me was as real as real could be.

It looked like it'd been forged with a mixture of different materials, the blacksmith folding the molten metal over and over until the finish looked the way ink did when it swirled in water. The result was a tangle of a million shades of grey and silver.

The plaque at the bottom of the case diverted my attention. '*This suit of armour is said to date back to the days of Camelot. Forged from a unique mix of cold iron, steel, and silver, it is believed to have been blessed by Merlin himself and intended to be worn into battle by Galahad, son of Lancelot.'*

I studied the sword that'd been placed inside the case and narrowed my eyes. It had the look of Arondight as I'd seen it in the vision the Codex granted me, but it wasn't the real thing. Somehow, I figured I'd know it when I finally saw it.

"Beautiful, isn't it?"

I looked up at the sound of a male voice, my heart leaping.

"The sword is said to be a copy of Arondight," he added. "It's not the real one, of course, but history tells us that Galahad was destined to wield it before it was lost."

He looked to be in his mid to late twenties, which made him a teacher or at least a staff member of some kind. He looked a little rumpled with his shaggy black hair, long-sleeved collared shirt, and a paisley tie that was crooked and a little loose. His black-rimmed glasses had fallen down his nose and he pushed them back up, the movement drawing my gaze to his chocolate-coloured eyes. If cute and awkward—with a twist of Italian heritage—was a thing, that's what this guy was. All the Naturals I'd met were glaringly Caucasian *and* British, but I was beginning to understand what a thousand years of evolution looked like.

"Oh, forgive me." He smiled and fixed his tie. "I'm Aiden. The librarian."

"You're a little young to be a librarian," I said, looking him over.

"You're a little too old to be a student, but who's judging?" He smiled and pushed his glasses up his nose again like it was a nervous habit.

"Does everyone know who I am around here?"

"Yes, unfortunately. That's what happens when you make a debut as grand as yours, Miss Ravenwood."

"Scarlett," I said. "Just call me Scarlett. And what debut?"

I was expecting him to mention something about killing a greater demon or being touched by Arondight, or one of my many other reckless accomplishments since becoming a Natural, but he came out of left field.

"No one throws Masters across a classroom with their Light and escapes the gossip mill." He smirked and nodded towards the armour. "Do you know much about our history?"

"I've been studying the Codex, but I'm afraid my head's all muddied with all the human variations of the Arthurian legend."

"Well, it's not all love and betrayal," Aiden explained. "No one remembers Arondight in the human stories—it's all about Excalibur."

"The Lady of the Lake gifted Arondight to Lancelot," I said, remembering what I'd read in the Codex. "So if Galahad was supposed to wield it, it was meant to have been handed down through their bloodline, right?"

"You've been putting a lot of thought into it, haven't you?" He looked impressed, which was a completely different reaction than I would've gotten from Wilder.

Shrugging, I twirled a strand of my purple hair around my finger. "I have a vested interest."

His gaze moved to my hair and he smiled knowingly. "Ah, yes, of course."

"You're a librarian and a historian by the sounds of it," I began. "What are your theories? What do you think happened to Arondight?"

Aiden's eyes lit up and I knew I'd asked the right question. Ask a historian about their tinfoil hat theories and they could go on for days about it. Except, it wouldn't be so outlandish now, would it? I'd come to expect anything from this world.

"Well, with Excalibur shattered and its power lost, the smart thing to do would've been to hide Arondight and keep its whereabouts secret. The fewer people who knew about it, the better. It only takes one possession for the demons to find a lead, and the world's greatest hope is done for."

The coin weighed heavily in my pocket. It was Greer's secret society theory all over again. If Wilder was right and I carried a piece of Arondight inside me, then did that mean my parents put it there to keep the sword safe?

To move forward with my search, I needed to decode the symbols on the coin, but could I trust Aiden? If he was compromised by the heaviness Islington felt after the breach and had been altered by

Human Convergence, then I could be screwing myself over before I even began. I had to be careful.

"The Naturals had just suffered a monumental defeat," he said, breaking through my thoughts. "They were splintered, separated across Britain, their greatest power broken. Their only hope would've been to hide Arondight until they could rebuild their strength. The fact that it was lost was merely disinformation to mask the truth." He shrugged. "At least, that's my theory anyway."

"But the Naturals never recovered enough to seriously consider facing the demons head on," I said. "And now I'm here…"

Aiden looked me over. "Yes, a mystery within a mystery. That's the double-edged sword of my line of work. Sometimes questions are answered with more questions."

"How frustrating."

"But it seems to me that Arondight wants to be found, don't you think?"

"If I knew where it was, then it'd make my life a hell of a lot easier," I drawled. "I don't want to be a famous war hero. I just—"

"Want to be free?"

My gaze snapped to his. I never thought of it that way before, but free from what? Expectations, uncertainty, the constant threat of life and death situations?

"Freedom comes with its own burdens," he said. "But that's life. You can't have the Light without the Dark."

I shook my head. "So you're saying the world will never see peace?"

"Naturals don't like to think of themselves as human, but we are." He blew through his lips. "Controversial, I know. We, as a species, will always be looking for something to fight. Rebellion is in our nature. War is our way of life. Peace is achievable, but a true golden age kind of peace? I think we'll always be looking for the next challenge, no matter what."

He made an interesting argument, and my head spun like a whirlpool.

"How are your classes?"

I blinked, his question brining me back to the present. "Sorry?"

"Your classes," he repeated. "It must be a challenge being the oldest student at the Academy. Is there anything I can help you with?"

"Uh… I suppose you could point me to the section on not assaulting teachers."

"That sounds like a good place to start." He laughed and gestured to the staircase. "We have a whole section on Light theory upstairs. There're some titles that may help with the basics. I can show you if you'd like?"

I grimaced. "Am I that transparent?"

"No, but you came to your Light later than most." He gave me one of those smiles that was genuine and open—the kind that made a woman's resolve crumble.

Could I trust him with the coin? Glancing at the suit of armour, I said, "I need all the help I can get."

"Then let me show you where to start."

I followed Aiden up the stairs and into the stacks, my gaze fixed on his back. Sounded like a good plan to me.

***

I poked at my chicken schnitzel, my appetite eluding me. The din of the kitchens was extra loud tonight on account of the headache I'd just chased with a couple of ibuprofen tablets.

Almost a week had passed since I'd arrived at the Academy and I hadn't found a way to settle into the student life. My new combat trainer wasn't impressed with my purple hue and drove me twice as hard as Wilder ever did, which was a feat in itself. The bruises on my bruises had bruises.

The chair opposite scraped back and I looked up as Wilder slid into it, dumping his plate down in front of him. He had the same bland salad and crumbed chicken. Obviously, his dietary choices had rubbed off on me.

"I heard you blew a teacher across a classroom." He raised an eyebrow. "That's your favourite trick, isn't it?"

My cheeks heated and I crossed my arms over my chest. "It was an accident... *this time*."

"So you're making progress on our mission in leaps and bounds."

"Nice to see you, too."

"Miss me?" He smirked and began to shove his

dinner into his face with all the grace of a starving lion.

"All the girls have crushes on you," I declared. "I can't see how when you look like that while you're eating."

"That'd be a first," he said with a smirk. "They all hated me when I was a kid. Best in my class and no girl asked me out."

"I can't imagine why. Your charm is *irresistible*."

"Speaking of… Yours is all the way up tonight," he said. "What's wrong?"

"I've got a headache."

"We don't get headaches."

"I get headaches." I waved him off. "I took something."

Wilder rolled his eyes and gestured for me to lean forwards. Reaching out, he tapped my temple and I felt his Light reach out.

"Should you be doing that?" I asked, frowning. "I don't think—"

"Better?" he interrupted.

I tilted my head to the side as he went back to his dinner. "Uh… yeah, actually."

"So apart from the reckless assault, how are your classes going?"

I shook off his nonchalance about curing my headache with a touch of his fingertip and replied, "Fine. It's the age gap that kills me."

"Age isn't important."

"Says the teacher." *Teacher*… Wilder would know something about the librarian. Hopefully he wouldn't ask too many questions in return. "Hey, what do you know about the history teacher in the library, Aiden?"

His brow creased. "The librarian?"

"Yeah. What do you know about him? He was very attentive the other night." Telling me stories and helping me find books. He'd hung around for almost an hour before leaving me to the pile of Light Studies tomes he'd picked out.

"Attentive? He must think you're pretty."

He may as well have stabbed a knife into my heart. "*Unlikely*."

Wilder snorted. "I know he has an older brother who's the full Natural package. Imagine that."

"*Imagine*." I rolled my eyes.

"You want to know what his family name is?" He waited expectantly, and I knew there was a punch line coming.

"What?"

"Thompson."

I choked on my spit and slapped my hands down on the table. "Thompson? As in…"

Wilder's eyes flashed and he laughed. "As in the guy whose arse you kicked in an attempt to defend Jackson's fragile honour."

"*Great*." Just when I wanted to get on Aiden's good side, he had to go and be Thompson's brother. Could I trust him now that I knew his family values? I had to figure out if he shared them before painting him with the same brush.

"What is it with you lately?" Wilder asked. "Ever

since you came back from the druidess' house, you've been angrier than usual."

He was seriously asking me that? "How's your best friend, Islington?"

"He's the same pompous twit he always was, but now he's the bloody headmaster."

"Sounds like your version of hell. Want me to throw him across the Academy with my Light? It's my party trick."

"*Scarlett*," his brow creased, "I showed you mine, now show me yours."

"I don't seem to be making any progress," I blurted. "For every new thing I learn, there's a thousand more I didn't even know existed."

Wilder shrugged, looking at me like the answer was simple. "You're too focused on the end game."

"I thought the end game was the point?"

"It's the battles leading up to it that make it the end game," he stated. "Don't forget about it, but focus on what you can do now." He raised an eyebrow. "Which is the thing about the you-know-what." *And deciphering the symbols on the coin.*

"You're right."

His lips quirked. "Any leads?"

"I can tell you who's in what clique, who rules the school, which guy all the girls fawn over, the outcasts, the bullies, and the bullied. What I can't tell you is if anyone has tangoed with the thing from the you-know-what."

He didn't look surprised, which meant we were in for the long haul. *Perfect.*

"Look, I don't know what's changed," he said, "but I'm… *glad*… we're talking again." He had to practically force out the word glad and my jaw tensed.

"Are you immune to happiness?" I demanded. "Or has someone put a curse on you, so every time you say one of the words listed under happy in the thesaurus, you get a blistering pain in that numbskull head of yours?"

"What?" he asked, glaring at me. "There you go again! Tell me what I did, Scarlett."

I glared at him, keeping my mouth clamped shut. I went to stand and his hand shot out and snatched my wrist.

"I know what happened," he hissed, keeping his voice low. "Jackson's loyalty to you is admirable, but it doesn't take much to notice when an area of the city opens itself up after decades of being closed for business."

I jutted my chin out and wrenched my wrist out of his grasp. "I don't know what you're on about."

"I know she's dead, Purples," he drawled. "I know that's what she wanted, so don't look so horrified. What I *don't know* is what she told you before she left."

"She didn't tell me anything," I snapped.

"That's a lie." He leaned back in his chair and studied me, his expression impassive. I couldn't get a read on him at all. "What I don't understand is why you stopped trusting me."

Because I opened myself up to you at the Necropolis and you saw everything, I thought. *You know how I feel about you and you've done nothing. Which means you either don't care or*… Or he never saw anything at all, and all this angst was one-sided. It made talking to him about it even more awkward and humiliating.

What had Arondight done to me? I access its power once and my hormones go haywire.

Everyone in this crazy world was in love with the wrong person. And it blew big time.

I knew I should tell Wilder about the coin and the things the druidess told me, but I couldn't. It felt like I'd already passed the point of no return. This was a puzzle I had to solve on my own, and Aiden the librarian was the only one who could help me sift through the symbology on the coin.

"Look, I don't know what I've done," Wilder went on, "but if it's something the druidess told you, then don't believe everything you hear. You know just as well as I do that words hold power, especially the riddles her kind spits out."

"The Druids are extinct," I stated. "*Truly* extinct."

"It's what she wanted," he repeated. "She knew she shouldn't have lived as long as she did."

"It was self-defense, but…" I shook my head. "She attacked me when I refused to take her life."

"She knew a lot of things," Wilder said, watching me closely. "It's safe to say she knew her end, too. It probably means she was waiting for something to pass before she could too."

I knew he meant me and Arondight, and I mulled over the words I remembered from that night at Seven Dials. The druidess said a lot of things in broken English, but one stood out enough for me to recall. *The future is unwritten, but the past holds all the secrets. All the power. Past losses, reborn futures.* If I unlocked the secrets hidden in my past, I could alter the future for the Light.

"Is that why you've been so angry?" he prodded. "Or is there something you're not telling me about the Necropolis?"

I froze, my dinner well and truly forgotten.

Wilder poked his fork at the salad on his plate. "That was some serious Light that flowed through you," he added. "It wouldn't be unexpected for it to mess with you at least a little."

"Ramona cleared me," I said, my cheeks flushing, but Wilder wasn't paying attention. "I'm fine. I just need to focus on controlling it."

"Again with the brush off..." he grunted and checked his watch. "When you're ready to talk about what the druidess said, you know where to find me." He rose to his feet, picking up his plate as he went.

"Actually, I don't." Honestly, I wasn't sure if I wanted to know where his room was. It was probably better than mine, which was just rubbing salt into the open wound in my heart.

"South wing, bottom floor," he said, flashing me a smile. "Last door on the right."

I made a face and picked up my fork.

"No more assaulting the faculty, Purples," he warned, walking away with a chuckle. "You don't want to get detention in this place, *trust me.*"

I watched his receding back, wondering what kind

of punishment Naturals got when they were naughty in class. Something juicy, I bet.

"Wait! What's so bad about detention?" I shouted after him. He didn't turn around, which only infuriated me more. "Wilder?"

5

———

In between studying and observing young Naturals in their native habitat, I visited the library every chance I got.

It was more reconnaissance on Aiden Thompson, than actual studying, but the Light books he'd recommended had helped. I hadn't accidentally assaulted any more teachers since the first day... though I was giving my new combat instructor a run for his money.

Patrick Frazier was a Scottish hunk who spent most of his time trying to beat instinct out of me in favour of regimented fighting tactics. He was great and all, but had nothing on Wilder. He'd driven me to breaking point for a reason, and now that I had the opportunity to train with someone else, I could see why.

The first few days were tough, but it wasn't long before I picked up on Patrick's methods and put him on his arse, much like I had Masters—but this time was deliberate.

I snorted at the irony, holding open the book in my lap entitled, *Your Light and You - A Study on Practical Applications for the Light Within*—at least I could pretend to take notes. I was nestled deep within the library on the second floor, overlooking the main staircase and the suit of armour below.

Your Light and You was dry as hell and not anywhere as good as *The Standard Book of Light*. Aiden's schedule wasn't that exciting, either. From what I could tell, he was meticulous about looking after the library and everything in it.

Despite the nerdy connotations, I was liking the quiet of the library. There weren't only books on Natural-esque topics, but a whole range of things that would usually be found in a human library as well—science, religion, art, history, and even a fiction section with all the latest YA blockbusters. Not to mention the crazy relics and weapons displayed all over the place. I wondered what it was like to be a Natural in the Middle Ages.

A cough sounded behind me and I jumped. Turning, the leather chair creaked, and I looked up at Aiden.

"You're here a lot," he said, raising his eyebrows. "Are you trying to escape the rigorous life of a Natural student, or is there something you want?"

"Books?" I offered with my best nonchalant shrug.

"You want to ask me something, but you don't know if you can trust me."

He just came out with it, and while it was refreshing, I almost choked on my spit. I doubted I'd make it as an MI6 agent.

"I…" I began, scrambling for a comeback.

He waved me off. "I have an affinity for reading people. I can pick up on their motivations. I also notice when students *linger*."

"Should I be worried?"

"That I'll get the wrong impression?" He laughed and shook his head. "Don't worry. I never do. *Anymore*…"

I got his meaning and felt my cheeks heat. A Natural librarian wasn't exactly someone the girls went wild for, not when there was an Academy full of combat training teachers and strapping young lads. Thinking about Wilder, I lowered my gaze.

"I don't blame you," he went on. "I gather you're constantly worrying about whom to trust, considering who you are."

"That's not all of who I am." I snapped the book closed, starting when a puff of purple Light burst from within the pages like a cloud of dust.

Aiden chuckled softly and took the book from my hands. "I know *Your Light and You* is dry as the Sahara, but you don't have to pour your frustrations across the pages."

"Is that what that was?"

"In a sense."

I groaned and rubbed my eyes. Studying was almost as draining as combat training.

"Would you like to go for a walk?" Aiden asked.

A walk? The notion seemed alien. "Don't you have to stay?"

"I'm not chained to the place," he replied with a laugh. "I can leave, you know."

"Okay then." I set the book aside and unfurled from the leather chair. How else was I going to figure the guy out? "Where are we going?"

He smiled and gestured for me to follow him. "You'll see."

Aiden lead me outside, holding the door open for me like a gentleman. Outside, the sun was lowering dangerously close to the horizon, signalling the end of yet another day.

We strolled across the gardens, weaving along paths lined with box hedges, until we reached the gate separating us from the unsculpted wilderness of the rest of the Academy grounds.

Ahead, I could see the outline of a building peeking out of a clearing. It was the ruined chapel Adelaide had pointed out on my day-one tour.

Until today, I'd never been inside. The crumbling façade was beautiful amongst the emerald landscape, the stone spotted with various grey and yellow lichens, and the cracks were stuffed full of spongy moss. Ivy had taken hold of one end, its vines clinging to the building like a life raft. It reminded me of the druidess' indoor garden and a pang bloomed in my chest.

"This chapel dates back to the early days of Natural occupation," Aiden said as we approached. "It was built somewhere around the year 1200, approximately one hundred years after the cataclysm."

"It's that old?" I asked as we stepped through the door.

"This was one of the few places the Naturals found refuge in those early days. It was here they were able to finally begin to rebuild what was lost."

Above, the roof had long since disintegrated, leaving the interior open to the elements. Our boots crunched on leaves strewn across the floor and we passed the stone pews that lined either side of the room. At the end, and behind the altar, a worn and crumbling statue of the Lady of the Lake crowned the entire room. Three large windows loomed behind her, now cast with a dense curtain of ivy and ferns. I imagined they'd housed elaborate stained glass at some point, but now this was a place of nature—and it seemed fitting.

"It's beautiful," I whispered, staring up at the structure.

"Religious worship was important to the Naturals of Camelot," Aiden said, his voice echoing off the stone. "We still adhere to the same beliefs, but we don't see prayer as an important part of our lives today. We uphold our personal devotions as we see fit."

"Much like the rest of the world," I mused.

I sat on the pew at the front, the stone cold on my arse. Aiden stood awkwardly, staring up at the statue.

"You know a lot," I said.

"I always liked knowing things," he said as he sat

beside me. "I always struggled with the more physical aspects of being a Natural."

He wasn't like his brother at all. There was no other way of putting it, Thompson was harsh, prejudiced, and an arsehole. But Aiden… he seemed intelligent, kind, and kind of shy.

"You never wanted to be a fighter?" I asked.

"No. It took me a long time to realise it," he replied. "I come from a family with a long line of decorated warriors. My brother's the Natural. I'm the disappointment they sweep under the rug."

"I doubt it," I said, attempting to console him. "Knowledge is just as powerful."

He didn't reply, and I supposed lots of people had attempted to convince him of the same thing to no avail.

"Islington said you came from the London Sanctum," he said finally. "That's where my brother's assigned. Do you know him?"

"Yeah, I…" I twirled a strand of hair around my finger, my cheeks flushing, "I kind of beat him up."

Aiden burst out into laughter. "*Good.*"

I straightened up. "Good?"

"He's always lording it over me. It's poetic justice."

"Uh… glad to be of service?"

"Were you worried it was going to dent my unwavering pride in my family name?"

"No." My gaze shifted to the side, a smile tugging at my lips. "Of course not."

Aiden smirked and leaned against the altar. "So what is it?"

"What's what?"

"What you wanted to ask me?"

"Oh, I…"

"You can trust me, Scarlett. I know you're looking for Arondight. Everyone does, so it's not that much of a secret. You want my help, is that it?"

He was right, but my other mission was burning a hole in my proverbial pocket. Someone at this school may or may not have been compromised by Human Convergence. I didn't sense anything demonic about Aiden, but that didn't mean much. Jackson's mutation went undetected for a long time before it became an issue and Wainthrope… Well, he was one step away from becoming a Vessel—*a willing host*—in order to achieve his ambitions.

"What would you do?" I asked. "If you found Arondight, what would you do with it?"

"I'd probably give it to you," he replied without hesitation.

"Why me?" I studied his profile, trying to puzzle him out. He didn't know me, and he'd just give our most sacred and powerful relic to me without thinking twice about it?

"Because it belongs to you."

I frowned, turning my gaze to the stone floor of the chapel. How did he figure that? I always thought the sword belonged to all Naturalkind, not just one person. I carried a part of its power within me, but that didn't automatically mean I owned the whole thing. The idea was absurd, and besides, I didn't want that kind of responsibility.

"Have you studied much of the Codex?" Aiden asked.

"A little," I admitted.

"Well, I don't know if you got to the part about Lancelot, but it tells the tale of how his bloodline was bound to Arondight, much like Arthur's was bound to Excalibur."

"Hold on," I said, straightening up and holding up my hand. "You think I'm descended from Lancelot?" I shook my head. That was too much, even for me.

"Perhaps," he replied, "or sometime in the last thousand years, your bloodline was also tied to it. That means Arondight is yours."

"Anyone can wield it," I argued.

"That's true, but no one else will be able to unlock its true power."

I grunted and suppressed the urge to roll my eyes. "Well, that's a bridge we'll cross if we ever come to it."

Aiden scuffed his toe against the stone floor. "So… did I pass your test?"

A laugh escaped from between my lips and I nodded. "A-plus, teach."

"Good. I haven't lost my grade point average."

I fished in my pocket and took out the coin, keeping my fist closed. "I found something and I—"

"Can I see?" He held out his hand and waited.

Something flared inside me and I knew I could

trust him. Was it my Light? I didn't know, but I handed him the coin.

I watched him turn it over in his palm and he studied it closely, his expression changing. He worried his bottom lip and my gaze followed the movement. Women looked over him for the muscly warrior type? What was wrong with them?

"It's not like any coin I've ever seen," he said, holding it so close I thought he was going to go cross-eyed. "I think it's more like a seal, or a token of some kind."

"A token?"

"It could be a number of things. A good luck charm, a symbol of membership, a seal placed on a shipment of goods. Those are called bale seals. They have the same kind of arrangement like on the back here. Four symbols denoting where the shipment came from and where it's going. Origin," he pointed to the first symbol, "sender, destination, receiver." Then he flipped it over. "This could be the symbol of the merchant or organisation to whom the shipment originally belonged to."

A shipment? Could it be from the case that once held Arondight? Why else would the druidess give it to me? I wish she would've told me who gave it to her, but knowing her kind, things probably went down exactly how they were meant to. After all, the reward was in the journey.

"It's very interesting," Aiden said. "There's not many of these in Natural history. It's a predominately human thing. Trading was big business back in the late Medieval period. The world was opening up and merchants were the new nobility. They needed a way to protect their goods and retain ownership en route to their destinations. Bale seals became as common as regular currency right up until the late eighteen-hundreds."

"So do you think this is a bale seal?" I asked. "Do you recognise the symbols?"

"I'm not sure." He turned the coin over and held it up to the fading light. "I'd have to do more research. Wherever it's come from, it's old. Where did you find it?"

"I, uh…" I hadn't thought of a cover story and I cursed my carelessness. The last thing I thought the druidess would want was for her existence to become common knowledge, even after she was gone.

"It's okay," he said, slipping the coin into his pocket. "I know we're little more than strangers, but one day we won't be."

I smiled and nodded. *One day.*

He rose to his feet and brushed off his trousers. "Can I walk you back to the Academy?"

"I think I might stay here for a while," I replied. "I have a lot to think about."

"Okay." He didn't seem surprised. "I'll let you know when I find something on the coin."

"Thank you."

The sound of his footsteps receded across the chapel, then faded entirely. My Light told me I was alone and I was glad I was becoming more comfortable using it. Greer was right in that regard—

the Academy was hard on me socially, but I needed the guidance to hone my abilities.

I stared up at the crumbling statue of the Lady of the Lake and wondered where she was. She was the bridge between where the twin swords came from and this world. If anyone knew anything about Arondight, it was her, but it wasn't like she was on speed dial… wherever she was.

All I knew was that I couldn't count on a mysterious magical entity who lived in a lake to tell me what to do next.

I'd been at the Academy for two weeks before I got the chance to call Jackson.

There was a bank of phones in old fashioned booths by the main office, and I slipped into one at the end. The others were empty, as was the hall. I could hear Adelaide the guidance councillor fussing over something in her office, but other than that, all the students were elsewhere.

I dialled Jackson's mobile number and scowled when it began to ring. I hadn't realised how attached I'd been to mine until I'd been forced to hand it over. There was no reason for a Natural to have a social media presence.

"Hello?"

"Hey," I said, instantly comforted by my best friend's familiar voice.

"Scarlett? I was starting to think you'd forgotten me."

"I've finally been given my one phone call," I drawled.

"And you used it on me?" he asked, mocking my tone. "I feel so special!"

"You're welcome." I laughed and nestled into the booth. "So, how are things back at headquarters? Any news on the you-know-what?"

"Ramona's still working on Barry," he replied, using the nickname he'd given his demon mutation. "It doesn't look like it's going anywhere anytime soon."

"Oh, Jackson. I'm sorry…"

"Don't be. Honestly, I kind of like it." He sounded sheepish and I clutched the receiver. "Is that messed up?"

"No," I murmured, "not at all."

"I mean, it's cool being stronger, faster, and having twenty-twenty vision, but I can do something good with it, too. I can help the good guys fight the bad guys for real."

"You don't have to justify it to me, Jackson," I said, smiling, "I get it."

"Romy and Martin found one of the names on your list," he said.

I straightened up. "Seriously? You should've led with that, you know."

"Sorry, but it doesn't really have a happy ending."

"Oh…" My shoulders sank, knowing that there was a point of no return. Wilder and I retrieved the information, but there was no way of telling when the 'subjects' had been infected.

"They brought the guy in, but he was too far gone for Ramona to bring him back," Jackson explained. "His humanity was gone."

I pinched the bridge of my nose. Every loss of life was a tragedy, and each one was just as difficult as the last.

"How many more are still out there?" I asked.

"Four, but that doesn't mean there aren't more than that."

"With the Balan gone and the lab destroyed, no more will be created."

"Until the alpha site is found. You blew up the beta lab, remember."

I sighed. The odds just kept piling up with each passing day, which made my anxiety about finding Arondight even more pressing. Not to mention keeping an eye on all these kids.

"What about you?" Jackson asked. "Have you found out anything about that coin?"

"It's taken a while," I admitted. "It's hard to know who to trust. If someone like Wainthrope could be turned, then everything and everyone's up for debate."

"But you found someone?"

"Yeah. The librarian, Aiden." Sweet, awkward, dorkishly handsome Aiden.

"Did I detect a girly sigh in your voice?"

"It's not like that," I argued. "He's nice, easy to talk to. Kind of like you in that regard." I snorted and rubbed my eyes. "Now that I think about it, you'd probably get along like a house on fire."

"Na, he's a book geek. He probably likes Dungeons and Dragons."

I slapped my palm against my forehead. "*Oh my god.*"

"Don't forget that coin is the one solid lead we have on Arondight."

"That's the one thing you don't have to remind me about," I replied.

"What about Wilder? Have you told him about it?"

I bristled, thinking about our argument-slash-discussion the other night. Wilder always knew when something was up, but this time I couldn't cave—it was too humiliating.

Jackson grunted. "Scarlett, you can't keep pushing him away."

"I'm not pushing him away," I argued, knowing full well that was exactly what I was doing.

"You're constantly picking fights with him to avoid inadvertently revealing your feelings."

Sometimes I wished Jackson would stop being the voice of reason in my otherwise chaotic life.

"We made up," he declared. "You didn't return my feelings, and yeah, it hurt, but if I didn't get over myself and realise that you can't choose who you do or do not love, then we'd never have made up. I'd still be out there and we'd never talk again. After all you've been through, do you really want that with Wilder?"

I always believed Wilder and I belonged together. As teacher and student. As partners out on the London streets. Fighting demons side by side. I knew I had to push aside the romantic feelings I held for him, but it was becoming too much to handle, especially after we'd merged our Light.

"He's the tough guy," I said. "The outcast who never fit anywhere. He's forever looking over his shoulder and doubting everyone's motives. He won't admit to anything."

"Reel him in, Scarlett," Jackson urged. "Tell him what happened with the druidess. You need to stop talking yourself out of it."

I didn't reply. I didn't know how.

Jackson sighed. "What are you thinking?"

"It's romantic, but there's something else. The way our Light reacts..." I took a deep breath. "Something deeper is going on."

"Does it scare you?"

My throat began to tighten as I held onto my tears. "*Yeah...*"

"Then you should tell him. He probably feels the same, don't you think?"

Maybe. Perhaps. *Doubtful.*

"Tomorrow," I said, my stomach churning, "I'll talk to him tomorrow."

6

I stood outside Wilder's room in the south wing of the Academy, my heart galloping in my chest.

What was wrong with me? I used to be able to tell him anything, *mostly*, so now shouldn't be any different. I raised my hand, hesitated, then knocked.

There was no answer, so I pressed my ear against the door and reached out with my Light. Immediately, I knew the room was empty.

The teacher's lounge was upstairs, so I ventured there before I lost my nerve. Movement ahead made my heart lurch and I swallowed hard. *Get a grip, Scarlett*. This was Wilder. Wilder... who I'd fought alongside. Wilder... who'd saved my life. Wilder... who's life I'd saved. Wilder... my mentor. I could trust him, despite the things I'd done... and felt.

Ugh. How was Wilder ever going to see me as his equal when I was constantly ranked below him? I could be as skilled as he was, but it wouldn't matter unless I had the official status to match. It was just the world we belonged in.

I was debating on rushing back to the dorms to do a nervous poo when I saw Greer standing in the teacher's lounge. Before I could make a hasty retreat, she spotted me lingering in the hall.

"Scarlett," her smile widened as I reluctantly stepped into the room, "I wasn't expecting to see you so soon. How are your studies going?"

"I'm a twenty-five-year-old high school student." I blinked, leaving the rest up to her imagination.

Her lips quirked and she nodded slightly. "Point taken."

We were alone, the emptiness making me shiver. The whole Academy had that chilly feeling the moment an area was emptied out of life. Considering demons were a thing, I wondered if ghosts were, too.

"Why are you here?" I asked, looking her over. She was wearing her official pantsuit and silk blouse, her sky-high heels adding a layer of sophistication that I bet men went crazy for. "Come to check up on us?"

"Yes and no. I'm here to give a lecture on the Codex. I do it every year."

"Oh."

"Are there any updates?"

I shook my head.

"Are you learning anything?"

I nodded.

"Good." She tucked a strand of blonde hair

behind her ear. "However, I'm disappointed no progress has been made on your mission."

"Kids are secretive," I said. "They don't like to talk to adults, especially ones who pretend to be one of them."

"Do you think Islington was overreacting in his assessment of the atmosphere here?"

I shrugged. "I have nothing else to compare it to. My stress could be masking it."

"Wilder has yet to give me his report. Perhaps he's had more luck. Have you two conferred?"

I shook my head. "We hardly have time to see each other. Our schedules are busy."

I could've sworn Greer looked satisfied, but it was so fleeting that I wasn't sure I'd seen anything at all.

"We're making some progress of our own back at the Sanctum," she said.

Jackson had told me as much, but it wasn't the good kind.

"How is everything with Brax and the Regula?" I asked. "I haven't heard anything for a while now. Not even the students or teachers are talking about it."

"That's the way we like it," she said with a smile. "The less common knowledge scandals like this are, the better."

"For security reasons? Or to protect young minds from forming their own thoughts?"

Greer narrowed her eyes, but didn't rise to my challenge. "Brax is making good progress with the Regula as far as I can tell. Jackson has been granted official leave to stay at the Sanctum and a full inquiry has been launched into Julius' dealings with the Balan demon."

"Will I have to give evidence again?" I made a face, remembering the grilling Wainthrope had given me.

"I don't foresee it, considering you're on assignment."

I was learning more about the Natural way of life every day, but when it came down to punishing criminals, I wasn't sure what they did about that. In wartime, humans tried people differently. I wondered if it was the same for us.

"What will happen to Wainthrope?" I asked.

"He'll likely be executed."

It was my turn to narrow my eyes. "The Naturals believe in the death penalty?"

"Of course we do," Greer stated. "We're at war, Scarlett. You don't think twice about killing demons, do you? They certainly don't think twice about killing us. We mustn't show mercy to those willing to betray the Light."

Hearing her talk so abruptly about life and death made my impression of her shift. Greer was sweet and intelligent, but she also had a dark side—the side that led her to work with Human Convergence all those years ago. Still, she was pure enough to touch the Codex, so what did I know?

"What does the Codex say about it?" I challenged.

"Julius sided with a greater demon for his own gain, conspired to murder Jackson, and to take you prisoner." She turned to the window and gazed down at the courtyard below. "You would request mercy for him?"

She had a point, but I wasn't sure death was the correct punishment for any Natural.

Closing the lid on that can of worms, I stood next to her. Below, a few students were crossing the yard, making their way to their next class or training session.

We spotted Wilder at the same time. Greer seemed to inhale a little too sharply, and I glanced at her out the corner of my eye. Was she *swooning*?

"What?" I had to go give her a poke, didn't I?

"He's changed," she replied.

"Who? Wilder?"

Greer nodded, her gaze followed him across the courtyard. "Wilder has begun to care again, and that's because of you."

Goody. I bristled, wondering if she was excited because it meant she had another shot with him. I wondered if that's why they broke up to begin with—Wilder's 'closed heart'. It wouldn't look good for the protector of the Codex to shack up with the insubordinate outsider, would it? Apparently, his stock had gone up in the last six months.

"I can sense your hostility, Scarlett."

I gritted my teeth and turned away from the window. When it came to confrontation, I was all over chopping down demons with swords, but not this. I didn't fight for the affections of a man. Either he loved me or he didn't, and Wilder couldn't be any less interested in a basket case like me.

"If you have an issue with me, the Sanctum, or your assignment, you're encouraged to speak up," she went on when I didn't make a move to reply, "professional or otherwise."

I looked at her, but she was cool as a cucumber. She was perfect, angelic, and a reminder of everything that made me uncomfortable with myself. Was she giving me an invitation to slap her down over Wilder? Or was it just her way of working out what my feelings were? These people had serious trust issues.

That was another problem. I still didn't see myself as a Natural. At least, not at my core. What made me different, a target, even amongst my own kind. It was hard to forget when my life was constantly at stake.

"I want to like you," I said, choosing my words carefully, "and sometimes, I do."

"I see," she stated. "I can hardly blame you. Leadership comes with certain responsibilities that make me... unlikeable."

It wasn't so much the leadership bit, but I didn't want to discuss that with her. I turned back to the window, but Wilder had already disappeared inside.

"Something else happened at the Necropolis, didn't it?"

I tensed at Geer's question. Report writing was something I didn't excel at, now or back in school. Then, I'd been half-arseing essays about the latest novel we had to read in English class, and now I was giving blow-by-blow accounts of how many demons I was slicing and dicing.

But it wasn't just my dislike of paper pushing that made me evasive. I'd left *a lot* out, but so had Wilder.

"I put everything in my report," I replied. "Not that it was my favourite thing to do. English was never my best subject. Is that the real reason you sent me back to school?"

"My reasons for sending you here are not nefarious." *That was a big word.* "If you have any issues, I hope you'll come to me with them. I'm not just a council member. Someday, I hope you'll see me as a friend."

A pang of guilt twisted my heart. "I will."

"I hope so." It wasn't a warning, not exactly, but I suspected there was more to her line of questioning than met the eye.

"I have to go to class," I said, eager to get away. "I'll see you later."

Turning, I began to walk away, my nerves totally shot. How was I going to tell Wilder about the things I'd been hiding from him now? The longer I left it, the harder it became, and now Greer was here. She was yet another wedge between us and she'd just told me that she wanted to be my friend. The leader of the London Sanctum, the protector of the Codex, the puppet master, the perfect woman wanted to be *my* friend? Was it really that simple?

Probably, but my feelings for Wilder had messed everything up.

"Scarlett?"

I stopped by the door and looked over my shoulder.

"I wouldn't trust anyone else with this task," Greer said. "These students are our future and must be protected at all costs. Remember who you are."

That last sentence was loaded with double and triple meanings. I wasn't just a student with a hidden agenda. To the Naturals, I was touched by Arondight. Little did they know, I carried a piece of it inside me.

"Way to stack the pressure on, Greer," I drawled.

She smiled, her stature reminded me of one of the portraits that hung on the library walls. "Good luck, Scarlett."

Obviously, I was going to need it.

I chewed on the end of my pen and stared out the window. Study period in super demon hunting school was just as boring as it was in human school. I'd been lumped into the senior class for the hour, which made it even more exciting. We were supposed to work on our assignments, but I was daydreaming instead.

I had a lot on my mind, but what else was new?

After running into Greer that morning, I'd been thinking about what she'd said to me. She suspected something was up with me and Wilder, and she was trying to get an admission out of me. She had him wrapped around her little finger, and I wondered what *he'd* said to *her*.

Then there was Aiden and the coin. I hadn't heard from him, either.

Aiden and Wilder—they couldn't be more different if they tried.

"She's giving a lecture on the Codex," Kayla was saying.

"Why do we never get to see it?" a boy, whose name was either Brett or Brad, asked.

"The Codex doesn't leave the London Sanctum," Trisha stated.

"Ever?"

"Only Greer is allowed to touch it," Maisy declared matter-of-factly.

"Have you seen it, Scarlett?" Trent asked. When I didn't answer, he waved his hand in front of my face. "*Earth to Scarlett.*"

I blinked and straightened up, my pen forgotten. "Huh?"

"Look at her… She's daydreaming about a boy," Maisy teased.

"I don't think about *boys*," I drawled. "I think about *men*. There's a difference."

Kayla's expression twisted and she threw a snide glare at Madeleine, who was bent over her Light Studies book on the other side of the classroom. It didn't take a genius to know a smart-arse comment designed to humiliate was incoming.

"Like Madeleine," she declared, "she's got a crush on Wilder. Poor thing. There's no hope for her."

I glanced at Madeleine, who'd shrunk behind her hair in an attempt to make herself smaller. I sneered at Kayla, my hackles rising. *What a bitch.*

"So it's okay for you to fawn all over him, but

when someone else does, it's pathetic?" I demanded. "Double standards don't work in the real world, Kayla."

"Luckily, this isn't the real world," she fired back. "This is about having the goods, Scarlett."

"Goods?" I lowered my gaze. "Are we talking about boobs?"

The other students began to snigger, which only served to enrage the beast before me.

"Just because you're older doesn't automatically make you wiser," she stated, her lip curling into an ugly sneer. "You grew up thinking you were a mental case."

I tensed. How did Kayla know that? She probably didn't, which meant she was fishing for a reaction and some ammunition. It was all about making up for her own shortcomings, after all.

I set down my pen and turned in my chair so I was looking at her right in the eyes. "I'd love to see you face off with a demon, Kayla… Because when you're staring down the throat of a twisted and rotting corpse, none of this petty shite matters."

She blinked at me, lost for words.

"And yes, I've seen the Codex." I didn't think I should tell them that I'd touched it, *twice*, so I flipped my hair over my shoulder and looked at Madeleine, who seemed awed I was talking back to the biggest bitch at the Academy. We were so alike, it hurt my heart—though when I was seventeen, I would've launched myself on Kayla and punched her in the face.

I guess I'd mellowed a lot since then.

Remembering my mission to infiltrate the Academy, I sighed. "What do you want to know about it?"

"Does it really shimmer?" Maisy asked.

"Yeah."

Kayla shot her friend a dirty look and she clamped her mouth shut, turning her head away. Guessed that meant I was still on the outer, then.

Greer wanted to know what my report was? These kids had a lot to learn about common decency and they were all set to graduate this year. It wouldn't be long before they were out on the streets, hunting demons and protecting the balance. If this was the best the Academy could produce, then they had a lot more to worry about than an alleged mutation. The balance was going to be toppled by a bunch of power-hungry mean girls.

Still, I had to find a way to be friends with them, otherwise I might miss the clues that could lead me to another suspected victim of Human Convergence. Greer was right, but these kids needed a huge reality check.

Glancing at Madeleine, I offered her a smile… but all she did was turn away.

7

Stratford-upon-Avon sat north of the Academy, nestled at the tip of the Cotswolds.

More famously known as being the birthplace of William Shakespeare, the little Medieval market village was now full of all modern conveniences—like 'big box' stores Tesco and Asda. A mall stuffed full of fudge shops, Shakespeare-themed souvenirs, cafés, and tourist photo opportunities sat in the centre of town.

I leaned against the outside of the Shakespeare Centre and watched the senior Light class wander the mall, looking for targets. Masters was eyeing off everyone like a hawk, making sure no one went off script. We were firmly in Natural territory, but that didn't mean demons weren't lurking amongst the unsuspecting public.

I couldn't believe the Academy sanctioned this. Practicing alteration—otherwise known as mind control—on unwilling humans was a little much for my tastes. Back when we first met, Wilder had been so nonchalant about it when he'd used it for his own gain, so I wasn't surprised the Academy took this stance. Anything flew in wartime, I guess.

After getting the lady in the café to give me a discount on my ham and cheese toasted sandwich, I was done. At least it wasn't a trick we could use on one another because that was another can of worms I didn't want to open.

"Hey."

I looked up at Madeleine, who'd appeared next to me. She'd been into the Shakespeare Centre gift shop by the looks of it. A crisp copy of *Twelfth Night* was tucked under her arm.

"Nice choice," I said. "Was that your assignment?"

"No. I made a lady to think she had toilet paper stuck to her shoe."

I raised an eyebrow and smirked.

She looked me over. "What did you do?"

"Got a discounted sandwich."

"Is that all?"

"Why is everyone always on my case about the mind control thing?" I huffed.

"Well you are…" She shrugged.

"I'm not a superhero because I'm purple."

"Would it really be so bad if you were?"

I snorted and turned my gaze back onto the mall. The usual cobblestones I was so used to in London were replaced with 1980s-inspired brickwork, but it didn't take away from the Medieval charm of the village centre. Thatched roofs were a thing here, along with matching black and white architecture, and old English signage. If I wasn't so concerned about possible demon possession—and mutation—I would have stopped off some place for scones with jam and clotted cream.

I supposed Madeleine wasn't far off the mark. It wasn't so bad being different when you were one step away from being 'the chosen one', but the pressure to be the person who swooped in and saved everyone wasn't something I was used to.

I could also see where she was coming from, considering the way the other students treated her. The one thing that was worse than being different, was wishing you were special, only to find out you were the same as everyone else. That's where Madeleine had it wrong—she was special just by being a Natural.

"Hey, Scarlett…" she scraped her hair away from her face, "I—"

A shout cut off whatever she was about to say, and I turned to find two grown men on the verge of brawling in the centre of the mall.

They weren't small guys—both were heavy and tall—and they had their hands fisted into each other's shirts. A woman was pleading with them to stop and I assumed she was the wife of one of them.

I saw Trent, Kayla, Maisy, and Trisha smirking behind the commotion. I pushed off the wall with a scowl, sensing Light all over the two humans. Intending to break it up before things got worse and we had a mall-wide brawl on our hands, I took a step forwards, but I didn't have to bother because Masters was already on the case.

"*Hey!*" He rushed up and shoved between the two men. It only took him a second to defuse the situation —I sensed his Light flare, and that was that. I could see why he was the teacher of the senior class, and a complete hard-arse.

"Walk it off," Masters 'suggested' to the larger man. The guy blinked and rejoined his distraught wife, who slapped his arm.

I glanced at Trent, who'd turned white as a sheet. This was his handiwork, and he'd just realised he'd gone too far.

Masters said something to the second man before sending him on his way. When he turned to the gaggle of students, his expression was pure anger. I'd never seen anything like it and underneath, I could feel his Light zapping and crackling like an overcharged Tesla coil.

"What's the meaning of this?" he demanded, throwing his hand into the air. A cone of silence fell over us, literally and metaphorically.

No one said anything.

"Anyone?" Masters demanded. "Trent?" He zeroed in on him, sensing his guilt.

The poor kid looked like he was going to keel over. "I-I—"

"*Well?*"

"I ah, I didn't… I…" He looked like he was going to puke all over the mall any second now.

I glanced between them and sighed. I couldn't believe I was going to do this… "Mr. Masters," I said, holding up my hand, "it was me."

He turned and his glare came with him. "Miss Ravenwood?"

"It wasn't Trent," I went on. "He's just trying to be sweet, but I don't want him to get into trouble on my account. I think I'm old enough to take the rap for my actions."

He looked me over with an air of skepticism. "You did this?"

"I got bored," I replied with a shrug. "I wanted to try some real world applications."

"Real world applications?" he scoffed, his face turning red. "Using your Light to incite a brawl is not the way we conduct ourselves in public. We do not risk exposure because we are *bored*." His voice rose with every syllable, and thankfully, we were under the umbrella of an illusion or we would be a spectacle. "You're being written up, Ravenwood!" He gestured at the other students, who were staring at us with wide eyes. "On the bus in ten minutes! Got it?" Masters stormed down the mall and climbed inside the Academy minibus that was double-parked in the loading zone at the end. The windows promptly began to fog up from the steam hissing out of his ears.

Trent turned to me, his gaze scraping the ground. "Scarlett… I—"

"Don't grovel," I snapped. "It's not becoming."

"That was pretty cool," Kayla said, dropping her usual hoity-toity tone.

"You're going to get into so much trouble with the headmaster," Maisy added.

"What kind of trouble?" I asked.

"She might get away with it," Trisha stated. "She *is* Miss Arondight."

I glanced at Madeleine and she scowled at me before storming off. I knew she thought I'd just sold out, but I had a mission. *Like that was an excuse.*

"There's a party happening down by the stream for the Spring Equinox," Kayla said. No one had even noticed Madeleine was even there, let alone extended an invitation. "You should come."

"Yeah, Scarlett, come," Trent said, wiggling his eyebrows.

"By the stream?" I asked.

"Yeah," Kayla replied. "It's behind the Academy, to the north."

"We're having a bonfire, booze, and music," Trent added. "Good times."

I'd just been handed the teenager version of a golden ticket. It was my way into the inner circle of cool kids, which meant my gamble had paid off.

"Cool," I said. "I'll check it out."

"Cool," Kayla echoed, then tossed her blonde hair over her shoulder before swanning down the mall, her entourage in tow, and climbed into the minibus.

Trent had stuck around and I narrowed my eyes. I totally got the kid versus adult divide now. I knew I could be reckless, but I had nothing on a horny teenager.

"Thanks, Scarlett," he said sheepishly.

"Just don't do it again," I replied, glancing towards the bus. "Just because we can influence people, doesn't mean we should use it. Do you want to get kicked out of the Academy?"

He shook his head. "It was stupid."

"Why did you do it?"

"I, uh…" he scuffed the toe of his boot against the ground, "I kinda like Kayla, and…"

He did it to get a girl's attention? *Sheesh.*

"There are better ways to get her to notice you, you know."

"She's the most popular girl at the Academy," he argued. "I'm nothing to her."

"You'd be surprised," I drawled.

"All the girls have the hots for the new teacher, *Mr. Wilder.*"

"Mr. Wilder?" I snorted and rolled my eyes.

"He doesn't have another name," Trent argued.

I scratched my head. Now that I thought about it, he was right. Wilder wasn't exactly first name material, but we did live in an ever increasing world where people made up their own creative spellings that had little to no basis on the English language.

"Forget about him. He's *old.* Practically geriatric." I slapped him on the back and turned him towards the minibus. "Besides, it's against the law."

"Aren't you supposed to be giving me advice?" he complained.

"There's a party coming up, Trent. Get dressed

up and tell her she's pretty. A girl like Kayla will lap it up, *trust me*."

"That's awful advice."

"No, it's not. She thrives on adoration. Compliment her until you've got her attention, then win her over with your stellar personality." Maybe that last part was a stretch, but it got him thinking.

"Really?"

I nodded. "What have you got to lose? If she says no, then you'll be right back to where you started, which is right here."

I pushed him towards the bus and sighed.

They were training to become soldiers in a never-ending war, but deep down, they were still kids. Kids with *hormones*. Light help us all.

***

Tick, tock, tick, tock…

The grandfather clock beside the headmaster's desk ticked loudly in the silence and the leather on the chair I sat in creaked as I moved.

Liam Islington sat in a grand chair behind his grand authoritarian desk, reading the incident report Masters had submitted the moment we'd arrived back at the Academy. I could see the angry pen strokes through the paper, and all the places the nib had broken through in his rage.

Wilder was draped in the chair beside me, clearly annoyed he'd been called into the headmaster's office. He and Islington were mortal rivals after all, but as far as I could tell, they'd avoided butting heads up until now.

"Scarlett," Islington said, lowering the piece of paper, "I'm extremely disappointed."

I looked at Wilder, but he didn't even lift his gaze and it stung. Either he was *that* bored, or he was hiding something. Ultimately, I felt like I was at a parent-teacher conference, though it was one where I'd have to come to my own rescue.

"I'm conducting a mission here, *headmaster*," I drawled. "I need the other students to trust me."

"By using alteration to incite a brawl?"

Wilder eyed me, half-confused, half-surprised.

"Yep." I popped the 'p' at the end and pouted.

"She incited a brawl?" Wilder asked, staring at me. "Scarlett?"

"According to Mr. Masters, she admitted to it."

"Damn right I did," I declared.

"Your continued presence here is defined by your behaviour, Miss Ravenwood," Islington said. "I will not treat you any different from any other student."

"Oh, come on," Wilder declared.

"Outside of your mission," he narrowed his eyes, "other than to teach you some much-needed discipline, I'm not sure why you're here," the headmaster said, staring at me with his cool, authoritative gaze. "Aside from today's infraction, and tossing Masters across a classroom, your grades are outstanding. Have you made *any* progress?" He glanced at Wilder then back to me.

I smiled. "I'm working on it."

Islington knew his hands were tied and leaned back in his chair, clearly annoyed. "If you disrupt the students any further—"

"Don't worry," I interrupted, "I'll try not to ruin their *fine* educations."

"Be thankful I'm not punishing you, Miss Ravenwood," he said. "I'm more than happy to if it helps you maintain your cover."

"Don't give her detention, Islington," Wilder said. "We both know you're itching to, but we need Scarlett out there with the students, wandering the boundary on pointless demon duty. If a threat does remain, it's inside these walls."

Islington's jaw began to grind and he set his gaze on him. "And what progress have you made, Wilder?"

"As we learned with the other cases, any alteration in the host can take time to manifest. Thus, we must remain vigilant and maintain our covers."

I tensed and shot a confused look at Wilder. Since when did Islington know about the mutations? I was farther out of the loop that I realised, but then again, I'd been the one pushing everyone away with my newfound surliness.

Islington clearly didn't like being schooled by his onetime rival. "Then you better resume your duties," he turned to me, "both of you."

I heaved a sigh of relief once we were out of the headmaster's clutches. At least I didn't get detention, that was something.

"You didn't do it," Wilder said as we walked down the hall. "I know you and you hate alteration."

I shrugged. Did he miss the part where Islington said I was excelling in all my classes?

"You're protecting someone else. It's not like you to be such a reckless show off."

"Does it really matter?" I snapped. "I needed a way in. I have to get to know these kids for their own safety."

"What's wrong?" he asked. "Are you ready to talk to me yet?"

"I just…" I glanced down the hall, but it was empty. No one was coming to save me from myself. "I just don't feel…" I shrugged. "I don't know how to describe it."

Wilder frowned, understanding crossing his features. "You won't be here forever, Purples."

"And what about you?"

"Neither will I. *Thank God.*"

I snorted and swallowed a smile.

We walked a little farther, emerging out into the main foyer of the manor. "You know, you're beginning to sound like me when I was your age."

"There's not that much of an age difference," I huffed.

"What are you getting at, Purples?"

Where should I start?

I scowled at him, doing my best to settle my churning stomach. "I know I've got a lot to learn—it's hard to forget when people keep reminding me—but I'm your equal, Wilder. I'm playing the role I was ordered to, but it doesn't mean I'm your inferior."

"When did I imply that?" He tilted his head to the

side. "You've made it crystal-clear that you don't need anyone to get by in this world, no matter how much you apparently need to learn."

I shook my head. I didn't want him to call me out on my bullshit.

"Separate the mission from whatever's going through your head, Purples," he murmured. "You're only a student on the surface."

"When this is over, when I've *graduated*, what'll happen then?"

"We'll both be reassigned."

"Where? Patrol?"

Wilder sighed and ran his hand over his face. "What you need to do is tell someone about what you did at the Necropolis. You need to come clean about your Light, Purples. Greer, Aldrich, and Ramona can help you."

My lips thinned. "What about you? You conveniently left your name out of the line up. Don't think I didn't notice."

His gaze darkened and his eyes flashed silver, almost as if his Light was calling to mine. "What good am I when you don't trust me anymore?"

His words cut through me with deadly precision and I jerked away from him.

"*Scarlett.*"

I didn't like it when he called me by my full name. It was the only time I knew he was being serious.

My hole had gotten so deep that I didn't know how to claw myself out of it. My own mess of feelings, secrets, and the lies I had to tell to keep them swallowed me whole. Honestly, I didn't even know how I'd gotten here.

Turning, I strode away from Wilder, climbing the stairs two at a time. If I was going to do anything, I was going to figure out if Human Convergence had stained the Academy, study the shite out of the ways of the Natural solider, then I was going to figure out why the druidess gave me that coin. For that, I'd have to go see Aiden in the library.

At the end of it all, I would be so formidable, I'd outshine Wilder, the wonder boy. The Naturals and the demons wouldn't see me coming, not by a long shot.

"Hey! Where are you going?" Wilder called after me.

"To make sure you never doubt me again."

8

Aiden pounced as soon as I walked into the library.

"You've had an eventful day."

"I see the gossip mill is in overdrive," I drawled as my cheeks heated.

"The students like to talk." He glanced around the library, but it was fairly empty on account of it being dinnertime.

"I was hoping you found out something about the coin I gave you," I said, changing the subject. "I could do with a pick-me-up."

"A few things." He gestured for me to follow him. "It's a real puzzle, you know."

"I'm beginning to wonder if that's what being a Natural is all about."

"Solving puzzles?"

"Yeah."

"Depends," he said with a chuckle. "There isn't

anything that cryptic about patrolling cities and battling demons."

It was my turn to laugh. "I suppose not."

"That coin was a beauty, but the way. I had to do some digital reconstruction, but I was able to clean the image right up. I'm still working on the text, though."

"Digital reconstruction?" I asked as he led me across the library to a door hidden at the back.

"Photoshop." He grinned and led me into what looked like an office in the aftermath of an explosion.

Papers and books were strewn on every surface and even stacked on the floor. Amongst the piles was an iMac computer, various stained coffee cups, and just a hint of Light coming from a display case at the back. Bookshelves lined the walls, and an old fashioned framed window let it the fading light from outside.

"Sorry about the mess," Aiden said as he cleared off a chair so I could sit.

It took him a while to find new homes for his research, so I turned my attention to the thrum of Light. The display case had a brass lock on it, and it was just as old-fashioned as the ones out in library— all lacquered wood and wibbly wobbly eighteenth-century glass.

Inside, I was surprised to see an arondight blade and promptly began to miss my own. The one in the case was much older, though. The hilt resembled more of a traditional sword with a heavy cross guard and pommel. Its blade must be huge when activated —which didn't sound dirty *at all*.

Aiden hovered over my shoulder. "Cool, huh?"

"How old is it? It reminds me of some hilts at the London Sanctum. You know, the retired ones."

"This is one of the earliest examples I've found," he explained, his eyes glinting with excitement. "The earliest use was recorded in the Codex around the year 1200. After the cataclysm, one of the knights of Camelot—whose name was Bedivere—devised a way to forge cold iron with steel in such a way that it created the Light-infused arondight blades. It took a while to perfect and he never saw them finished, but without Bedivere, we wouldn't have a way to fight the demons as effectively as we do now. This one was forged around the year 1350, but it's hard to tell."

"Shouldn't it be in a museum somewhere?"

"We don't have museums," he replied with a shrug. "The walls of the Sanctums and in the library are the only places we have to display our history."

I gazed at the hilt. "Shame…"

Aiden looked as forlorn about it as I felt. His historian side was really shining through, revealing just how much the Naturals had lost in the cataclysm.

"We can't afford to stop and ponder the past when the future is so precarious, I suppose." He patted the now empty chair and said, "I've found out some pretty interesting things about your coin."

"You have?" I slid into the seat as he woke up the computer from its swirling screensaver.

"See the flame here?" He showed me a high-resolution scan of the head's side of the coin. "It's a symbol for power and authority. If it's a bale seal like I suspect, then this is the organisation it ultimately belongs to, which makes deciphering this extremely important. But…" he clicked the mouse, zooming in on the image, "the more I looked at it, the more familiar it felt. Turns out," he reached for a hardcover book on the table, "there's a reference to it in the Codex."

"The Codex?"

"Yeah. Greer is here giving lectures," he said. "Maybe we could request that she consult the real Codex. If it's linked to Arondight, she'll definitely help."

My hackles rose and I shrugged. "Where's the symbol?"

"Here." He clicked onto another window on the computer and the twisting flame became sharper. "I was able to clean up the image so I could cross reference it with a digital copy of the Codex. The flame matches the one on this page." He handed me his hard copy of the Codex and tapped the illuminated drawing on the left page.

It was a Medieval-style image of a ring of standing stones in a dense forest with a night-time sky shimmering above. Runes were etched into the stones, similar to the ones on the Druidic runes the druidess had Wilder and me retrieve from that laboratory. Though it was the symbol on the rock in the centre that caught my attention. It was small, but it was there —the same twisting flame from the coin.

"Do you think these stones still exist?" I asked.

"Maybe, but they could be anywhere. Nature has a way of reclaiming places like these."

The text on the other page was in Latin, or some early form of English—it was hard to tell.

"What does it say?" I pointed to the text.

"It's gibberish, for lack of a better word."

"It doesn't say anything?" I frowned and held the book closer to my face like it would all suddenly make sense. "At all?"

"There are a few pages like that," he replied. "Many of them don't have cyphers. That's why I think you should ask Greer. The true Codex can sometimes reveal much more, especially when needed. There's so much Light infused in it that it takes a skillful eye to peel back all the layers."

It was so one of those moments, but I couldn't think of anything worse than speaking with Greer right now. Not after the mess I'd made with taking the rap for Trent and standing off with Wilder.

I ran my fingers over the illumination, the paper devoid of the Light that flowed through the real thing. I was letting my jealousy ruin my chance at finding my lost family and a clue to where Arondight might be hidden. I couldn't let a stupid crush be the reason the world fell to Darkness.

I'd explain it to Greer. As the protector of the Codex, she'd be able to consult it and help decipher the meaning behind the coin, the coded page, and the druidess' words. *The future is unwritten, but the past holds all the secrets. All the power. Past losses, reborn futures.*

Then I'd make things right with Wilder. He was too important to me to lose forever. He'd kept my secrets, concealed the truth about my affinity with Arondight, and how I'd destroyed Markzoth, all while I acted like a crazy hormonal teenager.

"Scarlett?"

Aiden was staring at me, his head tilted to the side.

"Huh?"

"Are you okay? You spaced out there for a moment."

"I, uh… I was thinking about stuff."

"Well, the mystery is just deepening." He shrugged and took the book out of my hands. "So far, I've only uncovered more questions."

"It's okay," I replied. "I'm really starting to get used to it."

Aiden laughed and shook his head. "I'll keep digging," he went on. "But you should really ask Greer."

I nodded. "I'll see what I can do." Right after I sucked it up and swallowed my pride.

Standing, I brushed off my jeans. "Hey, thanks for all your help with this. I couldn't have done it on my own."

He pushed his glasses back up the bridge of his nose. "You're welcome."

I decided to go see Greer before I lost my nerve, which was the moment I left the library.

As a glutton for punishment, I put my head down and ventured across the Academy to the rooms where I knew she was staying. Not so ironically, it was the top floor of the rear wing where the posh apartments were located.

Once upon a time, the owner of the manor would've called these rooms home. There was a private bedroom, dressing room, sitting room, music room, and various others that had no reason other than to rub wealth into visitors faces. Now, they hosted important visitors to the Academy. Visitors like Greer.

When I approached, I was surprised to find the hallway empty. I half expected there to be guards considering the apparent threat that lingered here. Perhaps she didn't want to raise suspicion and compromise our mission.

Ahead, the main door to the sitting room was ajar and I lingered as the sounds of a hushed conversation ebbed though the crack.

Knowing I shouldn't eavesdrop on the exalted protector of the Codex, I did the opposite and listened in. When it came to respecting authority figures, I liked to do the exact opposite—it made for a better plot twist if you asked me.

"I can sense it, too." I recognized the female voice. "Do you know why?"

"She's become distant." *Wilder.*

My heart lurched, sending a painful zap of

electricity through my body. I was frozen in place, knowing I should leave while the going was good, but too afraid not to. They were talking about *me*. Me and the giant hole I'd dug myself into. I'd be stupid not to think others had noticed, least of all Greer.

"What aren't you saying?" she demanded. "What are you keeping from us, Wilder?"

"*Nothing*. She's pushed me away. I'm just as in the dark as you are."

"No, you're not." There was some rustling and her voice came again. "You know she has feelings for you."

I almost died on the spot from an acute case of utter humiliation.

"And what do you want me to do about it, Greer?"

My heart stopped beating and I almost lost it. *Nothing*, I thought to myself. *Neither of you will do anything. God forbid you alienate your only lead on Arondight.*

"You should do what your conscious and heart dictates. I won't—"

"You know how I feel, Greer," he interrupted. His voice had taken on a husky tone, and I was unable to stop myself from peering through the crack into the room beyond.

I was just in time to see Wilder wrap his arms around Greer and kiss her. He held her in the passionate, unbearable, wild way I'd dreamed he'd hold me.

It was then that I saw the troll doll on the table

beside them, watching their passion unleash. *My* troll doll. The same one Wilder had given me.

I peeled away from the door and walked down the hall, everything inside me numb. My heart had ceased beating, my Light had frozen into a violet lump, and my hope had been shattered.

I thought Wilder and I had something special, but I hadn't tried to connect my Light to anyone else. What we did at the Necropolis probably wasn't special at all. It was all Arondight and nothing to do with me.

It was always about that stupid sword. In that moment, I hated it.

I turned a corner, putting distance between me and the scene of the crime. I knew it. I knew it all along, and so did Wilder. I was the one too stupid to see how it was going to end. He'd always love her.

It seemed the angsty high school do-over had come full circle. There was always the guy who broke the girl's heart, but unlike the Hollywood happily-ever-afters, this story was going in another direction.

I had another destiny and I had to face it on my own.

"Scarlett?"

I turned, my heart lodging in my throat. My hand reached for my arondight blade, but it wasn't there. I had nothing to worry about, though—it was just some nerdy librarian.

Aiden looked me over, his expression full of concern.

We were standing in a part of the Academy I hadn't seen before. A hidden corner full of musty curtains, paintings with creepy eyes that followed you around the room, and furniture that was covered in huge white sheets.

"Are you following me now?" It came out a little harsher than I intended and when he flinched, I melted. "I'm sorry, I…" I trailed off, knowing anything I had to say would sound lame.

"Are you okay?" he asked. "You seemed a little out of sync before, and now…"

If I was out of sync with my internal operating system before, then the whole thing must've crashed after what I'd seen. I'd never had a more brutal reality check in my life.

"Being a teenager was bad the first time," I replied with a shrug. "And the second time isn't much better, either."

"There's a metaphor in that."

"Something about leaving the past where it is, I suppose."

Aiden grinned and nodded.

"You're so awkwardly happy," I said, watching him closely. "What's with that?"

"If I knew, my parents would've beat it out of me as a child and I'd be at some Sanctum cutting down demons with an arondight blade, instead of burying my nose in a book." He drew in a deep breath, his long, rambling sentence really taking it out of him.

"It's not weak to play to your strengths," I retorted. "Not every battle is fought with a sword."

He looked me over with a skeptical eye. "Why are you at the Academy again? It seems like you've got all the training you need to go out there and battle the Darkness."

"I got the wrong type of education, I guess," I replied, sidestepping his question. I liked Aiden, but there were things about mine and Wilder's presence that needed to remain a secret. "They don't exactly teach kids how to use their magical powers in public school. Then there's the alternate history, which is a whole other kettle of fish."

"Ah, it certainly is fantastical to an outsider, I guess. Magical swords, demons, King Arthur, Lancelot…"

"Did it really happen like the human stories?" I asked. "Arthur, Guinevere, and Lancelot?"

"The ultimate love triangle," Aiden mused. "It certainly is a tragic story. Guinevere was bound to a king she'd never met, but she fell in love with the man sent to protect her on the journey to Camelot."

The only thing I could be certain of, was the fact that the story wasn't getting a repeat performance.

"What is this room?" I asked, changing the subject.

"Just a disused sitting room," he replied.

I narrowed my eyes, my suspicion rising. "How did you know how to find me?"

"I saw you walk this way."

"Oh…" If there was anyone altered by Human Convergence in this place, it wasn't Aiden. At least, I didn't think so.

"Are you happy, Scarlett?"

His question blindsided me and I stumbled over my thoughts before they ever reached my mouth.

"I guess I'm just uncertain of my position amongst the Naturals…" I replied. "I'm having an identity crisis."

"These things take time." He looked me over and must've sensed something more was awry, but he didn't press. Instead, he just shrugged and asked the perfect question, "Are you hungry? I'm going to get some dinner. I hear there's a lamb roast tonight."

9

———

I never bought into the depressive heartbreak spiral that people always went on about.

Ugly crying into a pint of beer and falling into a gutter on the way home, drunk dialling the guy who'd ripped out your heart and squashed it in the palm on his hand—those were all alien scenarios to me that belonged in the movies.

I'd always been tough, never showing anyone how I truly felt, but now I was all grown up. I was supposed to roll with the punches. Move on. Come to terms with the fact that Wilder loved Greer, not me. It wasn't meant to be.

Yeah, so I was never good at doing what I was 'supposed' to do. It felt like I had nothing to lose, which meant I was in the mood for some major anarchy.

Today was the Spring Equinox—the moment the sun crossed the celestial equator, or the imaginary line in the sky that marked the spot where the planet was divided into northern and southern hemispheres. It didn't sound that exciting, but the Naturals seemed to think of it like a miniature religious holiday. Not as important as the Solstices, but their version of a bank holiday. The only difference was that we didn't get a day off from classes. To counter it, the cool kids had organised their own party out in the woods.

I walked across the Academy grounds, the night sky stretching above me. A million pinpricks of light began to emerge the farther I moved from the artificial glow of the manor. It was a nice feeling being away from the city with its noise, pollution, and demon infestation. Still, the habits I'd picked up at the Sanctum hadn't quite left me.

It seemed like a good idea to stash my cold iron dagger—the one I'd smuggled into my room—inside my boot. In case of emergencies, of course. It rubbed awkwardly against my ankle, letting me know I'd grown soft over the last few weeks. Man, I missed my arondight blade.

Moving into the trees, the Academy disappeared and I had the eerie feeling of being alone in the wilderness, but a light ahead signalled that I was on the right path. So this was where the students had their secret parties? It was deep enough in the forest that the light was shielded from any wandering eyes of the Academy, and the noise was absorbed by the trees and a few tricks they'd placed around the party zone.

I could see various groups of Natural teenagers around a bonfire, laughing and dancing to music, and some were even doing tricks with their Light. A boy did a triple backflip from a standing position, making the others around him laugh.

I was just stepping into the clearing when Trent spotted me.

"Hey, Scarlett!" he called. "You came!"

I stood beside him and shoved my hands into my jacket pockets. "Of course I came. I need an outlet."

"Hey, thanks again for the other day." He smoothed down his shirt and cast a shy glance across the clearing to where I suspected Kayla was standing.

"It was your first and only 'get out of jail free' card," I warned. "But I can see you listened to something." I raised my eyebrow as I looked him over. "You got dressed up. Told Kayla she's pretty yet?"

His cheeks heated so much that I could see the flush in the warm half-light of the bonfire.

"You want something to drink?" he blurted.

"Kayla needs an alpha male, Trent. Shy is only cute for so long with a girl like her."

"Can you stop talking so loud?" he hissed, shoving a can of lager at me.

I turned the can around so I could read the label. It was cheap, but it was beer. Total contraband in these parts. "How did you get this?"

"You don't think we have ways of smuggling stuff onto the grounds?" He made a face. "I'm going to need one or two of these if I'm going to tell Kayla how I feel."

"What ways?" If someone could smuggle in beer,

then it wasn't much of a stretch to smuggle in a mutation, either.

"That's a trade secret," he declared, wiggling his eyebrows.

I snorted and cracked the top of the illegal alcohol open, knowing I'd get it out of him sooner or later. He obviously wanted me as his wing-woman.

"Scarlett!" Kayla was waving at me across the bonfire. "Scarlett, come here!"

I gave a pointed look at Trent. "Now's your chance, big shot. Step one, tell her you think she's pretty."

"Shut up," he grumbled as we rounded the fire pit.

Someone had hooked up a beat-up iPod—by the state of it, the thing was a relic—to a speaker, and it was playing a random shuffle of music—rock, pop, electro, hip hop, and more. The dulcet tones of Eminem belted out across the forest telling us how we had to lose ourselves in the moment. *If only...*

Kayla was sitting on a fallen log with her usual group of hangers on, Trisha and Maisy. A few other students were hanging around, and I'd even started to remember some of their names—Max, Andy, Fiona, Rhiannon, Grant, and Harriet.

I sat on the log amongst the popular kids, wondering how my life had led me here.

"Maisy thought you weren't going to come," Trisha said as I wiggled my arse into a comfortable position.

"*Trisha,*" she whined before she turned to me. "All

I meant was that we're so much younger than you. I thought you'd be bored."

I made a face. There they went with the ageism again.

"I wouldn't miss seeing how Naturals like to party," I declared. "I missed out on all this stuff growing up. I only got the human version."

"They don't teach you how to slay demons at regular school?" Trent said with a smirk, making everyone laugh.

"Your parties aren't that much different from human ones, though," I said. "Apart from the Light thing, you've got all the markers."

"What markers?" Trisha asked.

"Music, booze, and hormones."

Everyone started to laugh again, which was more of a reaction than I ever got at their age. I'd have to be invited first, but the only parties I'd ever gone to in high school were the ones I gate crashed. Did this mean I was in?

"I bet they didn't do this at your human parties," Trent said, holding out his palm. A burst of silver Light manifested, shooting up into the air and exploding into little fireworks.

Kayla grinned at him, batting her eyelids. "You're so good at that."

"Tricks are Trent's thing," Maisy told me. "He's always figuring out new things."

I was starting to see that, but tricks weren't going to get him far with a demon. I supposed I couldn't blame them for having some fun. What was the point of having bad arse powers if you couldn't make a little firework now and then?

"Hey, can you show me how to do that?" I asked, elbowing him.

"Yeah!" Trisha cried. "I'd kill to see some purple fireworks!"

"I didn't even know we could do shite like this," I said. "It's all work, responsibility, seriousness, life or death out there."

"We can do tons of things," Trent declared. "You've gotta know your limit, though. If you push too hard, you can eat into your soul."

"And that's bad," Kayla finished for him.

"I've been soul sick before," I told them, much to their shock. "I didn't know what I was doing and…" I trailed off, not knowing how much I should say.

"And what?" Kayla demanded.

Everyone was staring at me and it was a strange feeling being the centre of attention. I wasn't sure if I liked it.

"I got into a fight with a demon," I explained. "I didn't have anything else to fight it with, so…"

"*No way*," Trisha whispered.

"You maxed yourself out fighting a demon?" Trent asked, gaping at me.

"I didn't kill it, I mean, I couldn't with just Light, but… *Wait*…" I glanced around the little huddle of students, "have none of you seen a demon before?"

"Well…" Kayla began.

"I saw one junior year," Maisy stated.

"My sister is at the New York Sanctum," Trisha added. "She tells me stuff if she can."

Wow. This school was more messed up than I realised. I supposed when they did finally see one, they'd hopefully know how to spot it and finish it off.

I decided taking a long draught of my cheap arse beer was better than going down that rabbit hole tonight. I was here to blow off some steam, not add to it.

Elbowing Trent again, I asked, "Okay, how do I make these fireworks?"

He gave me a crash course, explaining how he shaped his Light, careful to tell me not to use too much juice. I was well-known for throwing Masters across the classroom, so the last thing we needed was an indigo forest fire.

I cracked my knuckles and assumed the position. "Okay, wish me luck."

I held out my hand and called on my Light, trying not to be too heavy-handed. I formed the little sparklers in my palm, then willed them to fire.

Purple sparks fired into the air and exploded into hundreds of little stars. They floated gently to the ground, fading as they went. Everyone turned to watch, pointing at the spectacle.

"Wow!" Kayla clapped. "You're so good at it, Scarlett!"

I watched my Light sizzle and pop, my eyes wide. It was beautiful and I wondered why no one ever took the time out to marvel at the gifts we'd been blessed with. There was so much darkness out there that we couldn't lose sight of the things we were fighting for.

After a while, the group splintered off, and I wandered around the bonfire saying hello to the other students. They were mostly seniors, but a few juniors had snuck out to enjoy a little contraband. I received a few wary glances, but no one was in a hurry to hide from me. It wasn't like I was going to tell on them—I needed this party just as much as they did.

I could really see the parallels now that I'd been on both sides of the teenage divide. Things were easier for the kids who were a part of the in-crowd and anyone outside of it was doomed to be miserable. Man, I really hated this hierarchy of cool bullshite.

I'd just finished my can of lager when Trent sidled up beside me.

"I thought you'd be in a bush with your tongue down Kayla's throat by now," I said.

"*Scarlett*," he moaned. The firelight flickered across his anguished face and I was having a hard time not feeling sorry for the kid.

"What? Where is she? I thought this was going to be the night you told her."

"I don't know how to say it."

"There isn't one way to say anything," I replied, slapping him on the shoulder. I wasn't sure if I was the right person to give him advice right now, but at least someone had a chance at a little romance. "You just tell her with whatever words you can."

He sank onto a tree stump and took several deep breaths. "I just need to work up some courage."

I sat on the ground next to him, watching the fire flicker and spark. I couldn't even tell Wilder how I felt about him, and now he'd gone and rekindled his love affair with Greer. She was more his match than I'd ever be.

I ground my teeth together. She'd even had the audacity to thank me for making Wilder care again. She was all like, *thanks for doing all the work and opening his heart for me, Scarlett, now we can go make Natural babies together*. Excuse me while I went and threw up.

I was so clueless about everything. It wasn't just Natural stuff. I mean, I was too stupid to realise I was manifesting magical powers. How could I miss that?

I glanced at Trent, who looked like he was about to do a giant nervous poo.

"Hey. What's it like to manifest?" I asked. "I mean, like *really* go through it."

He shrugged, obviously glad for the distraction. "It's different for everyone. Some people get really sick, others don't really feel anything. Sometimes kids accidentally blow things up. It can be triggered by a traumatic event or it could be a hormonal change. Kids can manifest anywhere between eight and nine, right up until fifteen or sixteen. The later you get your Light, the less likely you'll come here, though."

"Hmm," I muttered, my mind mulling over it. I wondered when I'd manifested. It could've been amidst any one of my many panic attacks. "It sounds like how the X gene manifests."

Trent straightened up, the glimmer in his eyes

giving away he was a comic book fan. "You like the X-Men?"

"I've seen all the movies, but I'm not sure that counts. My best friend, Jackson, is into all of that stuff—he's a professional gamer."

"No way! That's *epic*."

"What a world we live in, huh? Demons are trying to bring about an apocalypse and playing video games is a legitimate way to make a living."

"It must be great being human," he said, taking me by surprise.

"Why would you say that? You've got magical powers."

"Yeah, that we have to hide. Humans get to be anything they want."

I hesitated, a pang of hopelessness tugging at my heart. These kids only had one path they could follow. They were born to be drafted into war and nothing else.

I wasn't sure it was such a great future to aspire to, which made it even more important that I find Arondight. It wasn't just about saving the world, it was about giving these teenagers a life where they could choose who they wanted to be.

I opened my mouth, but I didn't know what to tell him. This was our burden and that was that. We were the only ones who could stand against the Darkness.

"You should tell Kayla how you feel," I said. "If she doesn't feel the same way, then at least you'll know. It's better than what you're putting yourself through right now."

Trent sighed. "You're right. We're graduating this year. I've got to man up."

I thumped him on the back. "That's the spirit."

He looked around the clearing, his confidence fading into a frown. "Can you see her?"

I stood and scanned the surrounding faces, but Kayla wasn't anywhere. "No, I—"

A scream tore out of the night, shredding through the music and causing everyone to stop and stare at the darkness. Trent rose to his feet, but no one moved as the sound echoed.

Me? I didn't hesitate. Dropping my empty can, I sprinted into the shadows… directly towards the danger zone.

10

The scream echoed through the clearing and I didn't hesitate.

I was vaguely aware of the other students falling silent, their heads turning towards the sound as I broke through the tree line. My boots crunched on fallen leaves as I legged it down the path to the stream.

The water bubbled and trickled, all it's quaintness suddenly too loud in the silence. Using my Light, I sensed someone up ahead—another Natural.

I picked my way over the uneven trail, searching for the student. Clouds had skidded across the moon, obscuring my vision and darkening the night. I wished I hadn't skipped over the enhanced sight lessons.

When I rounded a bend, I saw them. A dark lump was heaped at the foot of a tree, prone and unresponsive. A shock of blonde hair caught the moonlight and my breath caught.

Kayla.

I fell to my knees beside her and pressed my palm against her forehead. Her skin was clammy to the touch and her temperature was spiking. I could feel it radiating off her in waves. There was no blood or any visible wounds, but it didn't mean she was going to be okay. Something else could be lurking out here. Something *Dark*.

My thoughts instantly went to Trent, but he was back at the clearing—he couldn't have done this. None of the students could have. As far as I could tell, no one had left the clearing, not until we'd heard Kayla's scream. But then who?

Sensing movement behind me, my head jerked up, but it was only a group of students who'd followed my mad dash into the woods. I was surprised to find it was Trisha, Maisy, and Trent. Maybe they had spines after all.

"Oh my God," Maisy cried when she saw her friend leaning against the tree.

"Kayla?" Trent hovered over me, panic clear in his features. "What happened? Was it a demon?"

"If it was a demon, the alarms would've gone off," Trisha stated.

Before they could descend into chaos and appoint a mob leader, I stood and shoved Trent down beside Kayla.

"Stay with her," I ordered. Turning to the others, I assigned duties. "Maisy, go back to the main building and get help. Trisha, go back to the party and make sure everyone stays put until the teachers get here. Use your Light if you have to. If something's out there, we don't want anyone else wandering off and getting attacked. Got it?" They stared at me, completely dazed. "*Go!*"

The two girls sprung into action, sprinting off towards the clearing.

"What are you going to do?" Trent asked.

I whipped my dagger out of my boot. "I'm going to do a sweep of the area."

His eyes widened when he saw the blade in my hand. "But you're a student," he argued. "What about Kayla? What if they come back?"

"Trent," I slapped my hand onto his shoulder, "you've been training for this your whole life. You already know what to do."

He swallowed hard and nodded, turning his attention back to Kayla. Other than the slight rise and fall of her chest, she hadn't moved.

I took a step back as I felt his Light flare. I gasped as a curtain of silver strands lowered over the pair, the shimmering tendrils shielding them from harm. The way it fluttered and settled over the two teenagers was beautiful, the glow pulsing in the ancient forest.

That was all it took for me to realise that Trent didn't just like Kayla—he loved her.

I felt a pang of jealousy but stopped it before it reached too far. Shaking my head, I brandished my dagger and forged into the darkness.

There was a lot of leaves and debris on the ground, which made my progress slow. If something was still lurking out there, I didn't want them to hear me coming. I could've used my Light to dampen the crunch of my progress, but I wasn't sure if whatever had attacked Kayla would be able to sense it. It was probably best to rely on the basics at a time like this.

Damn, I really wish I had my arondight blade. Whatever this thing was, it was too smart to be a lesser demon. If it was a mutated super demon or an Infernal, the most I could do with my Light was give it a zap, and stabbing it with the dagger would only annoy it.

Could I rely on my little shard of Arondight? I wasn't sure I could take the risk. I mean, I hadn't tested it out since the Necropolis.

Back-up was coming, I just had to play it cool.

The forest thickened farther downstream, the trees reaching over enough to make a dense canopy. Silver light was filtering through the branches, creating little moonbeams that danced across the darkened shadows.

I could sense movement all around. Animals stirred in the distance, fish swam lazily in the stream, an owl hooted as it hunted for its dinner, and the footsteps of a small red fox rustled as it lurked in the underbrush.

It wasn't long before I felt out the outer edges of the Academy grounds, the barrier warding this place from the human world buzzed like a live electric fence. But there was something off about the way the sound reached me…

I kept moving, scanning the forest and making sure my grip was tight around the hilt of my dagger. I took another step and the taste of copper filled my mouth. Gagging, I spat, but it was still there. I remembered the demonology teacher talking about the various effects demons had on Naturals—rank smells, sounds, vibrations in the air, hallucinations, *taste*. They could all be hallmarks of something Dark.

The taste faded as I caught sight of a clearing ahead. A branch snapped, the sound echoing through the stillness and I froze. The sound came from ahead and my heartbeat sped up as I realised the predicament I'd gotten myself into.

I was alone in a dark forest, with a demon lurking in the shadows, and all I had was a dagger. *Good going, Scarlett.*

Movement pulled my attention forwards. One step to the right and I saw them. Two figures stood in a clearing, talking intently.

Inching forwards, I leaned against the trunk of a tree and peered around the snarl of bark. One figure was shrouded and the other was standing in a shaft of moonlight.

It was a boy, a student by the looks of him. He was just a kid and his body had been overtaken by an Infernal. I could sense its stink from all the way over here, the rasp in its voice was a giveaway as was the silver flash in its eyes as he turned.

The other figure was harder to make out. Wreathed in Darkness and shadows, the only thing I could tell about them was that they were something *more*. I remembered what Markzoth looked like, and it was nothing like this. He was a shadow inhabiting a body made up of stitched together body parts, but this creature seemed to be whole in a way the greater demon hadn't been.

Tall and slender, the figure was nothing more than a shadow, an inky stain on the surrounding forest. It was using its power to conceal its identity, even from the Infernal that stood before it.

Was this the mutated Natural we suspected was lurking on the Academy grounds? If it was, it was nothing like Jackson. Maybe we were too late… or maybe it was something else entirely.

"You were reckless," the Infernal hissed. "*Recklesssss…*"

"She deserved it," the creature replied. Their voice was so twisted, I couldn't tell if it was male or female.

"Scarlett Ravenwood is here. The one touched by Arondight."

The creature scoffed, "She's pathetic. She can't even control her Light. She's no threat to us."

My mouth fell open. Pathetic? I killed a greater demon! If I had my arondight blade, I'd teach them a thing or two.

"They already suspect we have infiltrated their school," the Infernal said. "Now they will have evidence."

"I'll handle it," the shadow replied. "You gave me this power so I could stand up to them. That's what I did."

"*Recklesssssss!*" the Infernal hissed, bearing its teeth at the creature.

Before I knew what was happening, the shadow

creature raised its hand and slashed at the demon, tearing the boy's throat open.

The boy let out an unearthly wail, the demon inside him shredding his vocal chords. The creature pulled away, then leapt across the clearing and through the tree line to the northeast. The Infernal roared and dragged itself south, away from my position in the west.

I had one second to make a choice… and I chose to go after the Infernal.

Leaping into the clearing, I sprinted towards the demon. He writhed on the ground, blood gurgling in his throat. I stood over him and silver eyes flashed as they met mine, his lips curving into a bloody grin.

"There you are!" it exclaimed. "Scarlett Ravenwood. *Too late*."

"I won't let an innocent boy die because of you," I snarled.

It began to laugh hysterically. "You'd save one when you risk the lives of many?"

"*Every life matters.*"

"You ran after the wrong demon." It bared its teeth and used the last of the boy's strength to lunge at me.

I plunged the cold iron dagger into its chest with a cry, forcing the body back onto the ground. The boy's mouth gaped as a plume of black smoke poured out of him, his chest rising off the forest floor and his arms flailing.

I slapped my palm over his throat, and blood seeped through my fingers at an alarming rate. I forced my Light into the wound, willing it to seal shut as the Infernal swirled in a confused tornado above me. The pulse of blood seemed to slow and I lifted my palm. A torn gash still gaped across his throat, but he was out of danger… *for now.*

The Infernal crackled and righted itself in a whoosh of static electricity. I'd excised it from the boy, but now I was completely exposed.

Holding up my hands, I called on my Light, and the cloud of smoke began to emit its own little electrical storm in response.

"I know you can hear me," I snarled. "If you've done anything to that kid, I swear I'll make it hurt."

The Infernal expanded and contracted. I supposed that meant it was angry. It was hard to tell what a swirling cloud of putrid black smoke was feeling, let alone saying.

The clearing began to glow with a dull shade of indigo as I gathered my strength. I was able to kill Markzoth with a zap of my little slice of Arondight, so why not a lower demon? There was only one way to find out.

"You know who I am," I taunted. "You know what I did in the Necropolis."

The Infernal flared, sparking and swirling.

"Don't think I can't do the same to you, because I can," I warned. "I don't need an arondight blade to send you back to Hell."

The Infernal flew at me and I dodged to the side, throwing a blast of Light at it. I missed and got a tree instead, the bark cracking and exploding in a shower of splinters. Cursing, I readied myself as the demon came back for seconds.

It rushed at me with incredible speed and my foot caught on the uneven ground. I fell, landing hard on my arse. The Infernal kept coming…

An arondight blade sparked over me and sliced through the cloud of smoke. It burst into flame, the heat burning my cheeks, and I was forced to shield myself with my arms.

Please don't be Wilder, please don't be Wilder…

"I can't say I'm surprised, Purples," he said, his surly tone not surprising. "You do have a knack for running headfirst into danger. We have to do something about getting you de-magnetised."

I groaned, my face flushing from more than a demon fireball, and sat up.

"You know, it was stupid to go after it on your own. It could've possessed you, then we'd all be screwed."

"It can't possess me," I stated. "Arondight protects me."

Wilder snorted as if he knew I was bluffing. "I'm sure they said the same thing the day of the cataclysm."

Pursing my lips, I climbed to my feet and dusted off my aching arse. I turned towards the boy, but he was just as I'd left him, knife and all.

"Do you know the kid?" Wilder asked.

"Not really. He's in one of the junior classes, I think." I looked at the dagger sticking out of his chest and couldn't stop the pang of despair. He was barely fifteen and now—

"He'll have to get tested," Wilder said, kneeling over him.

"His throat—"

"You stopped the bleeding, Purples. He's going to live."

A commotion in the forest broke through the still night and I spun on my heel just as three Naturals appeared—my combat instructor, Scottish Patrick, then Masters appeared out of the gloom, followed closely by Adelaide. They all had their arondight blades in their hands, ready to fight.

"Hell," Masters cursed as he saw the kid on the ground. "That's Stewart Granger."

"Poor boy." Adelaide knelt next to him and checked his temperature. "He's burning up."

"He needs to go to the infirmary," Patrick said. "What was it? It stinks like an Infernal."

"Yeah," Wilder said, eyeing me. "It was a particularly nasty one."

"I'll take him," Masters said as he picked up the boy. "You should sweep the rest of the grounds. It mightn't be alone."

"What about Kayla?" I asked. "She was in pretty bad shape. I don't know what it did to her, but she was out cold."

The other teachers looked at me as if they were seeing me for the first time. None seemed surprised that I was here, but there was too much going on to ponder the *why*.

"One of the other instructors has her, Purples," Wilder said. "You should go back, too."

"But—"

"I know you want to help, but you're unarmed and we need to protect you, too." He gave me a stern look before turning towards the dark forest.

Patrick and Adelaide had already moved off, and I could hear their footsteps crunching as they passed through the trees.

I grabbed Wilder's arm, my skin zinging from the contact. He narrowed his eyes, but didn't pull away.

"There was someone else out here," I whispered. "A dark shadow. I couldn't get a good look at them, but I think it was a mutated Natural."

He tilted his head to the side.

"I've never seen anything like it," I said, answering his unasked question. "And I haven't learned about it in any book. It wasn't anything like Jackson, it was… *more*."

Wilder nodded, his gaze searching mine. "I'll keep an eye out."

I stared at him, but all I could see was him and Greer locked in a passionate embrace. I jerked my hand away and took a step back. Wilder frowned, his eyes flashing silver in the half-light.

"No heroics," he said. "Go straight back to the Academy. Being the reckless hero is my cliché, and I can't have you stealing my title."

"Wilder…"

"Go," he said. "Those kids trust you. If you're lucky, they might even look up to you now."

He was right. As much as I wanted to go out into the world and fight, there were other battles that needed warriors. Tonight, I had to go make sure the queen bee of the Academy was okay.

"Am I going to get into trouble over this?" I asked.

"For running headfirst into danger with only a contraband dagger to protect yourself with?" Wilder smirked. "Of course you are, Purples."

Great, it looked like I was finally going to find out what Natural detention looked like.

Turning, I made my way through the forest and back towards the lights of the Academy. Somewhere in the darkness behind me, Wilder and the others were searching for a shadow that may or may not be the mutated student we'd been sent here to find.

A part of me was hoping it wasn't true, that we were worried over nothing, but I'd seen it. It knew who I was and how much I sucked at Light studies. The Academy was in deep shite.

11

———

I was becoming intimately acquainted with the *tick tock* of the grandfather clock in Islington's office.

I stared at the hands as they flicked to midnight, the chimes filling the tense air with their metallic clanging. Turns out deep shite was pretty deep in these parts. Behind me, I felt Islington's enraged stare burning a hole into my back. Adelaide sat in an armchair on one side and I sensed Wilder somewhere.

Outside, the night seemed darker, but it might have just been the lights of the office dampening everything on the other side of the wibbly wobbly glass. I wondered if anyone else thought the cold, damp, mothballed stench of this place was annoying. I supposed they got used to it after a while.

I didn't know why they were so angry. If I didn't go after the Infernal, that boy would have died and who knew who else it would have infected. I also got visual confirmation that something was trying to infiltrate the Academy. A 'good job, Scarlett' wouldn't go astray.

"You could have gotten yourself possessed," Islington said, breaking the uncomfortable silence. "Then our only connection Arondight would have been lost."

I swallowed my anger and turned. I looked to Wilder, but he gave a soft shake of his head—he hadn't found any trace of the shadow.

"You're lucky Greer isn't here," Islington fumed.

I sucked in a sharp breath. "She's gone?"

"She went back to London this afternoon," Adelaide explained.

Nice of someone to tell me. But then again, I wasn't exactly a priority when it came to need-to-know information. I guess I'd have to find another way to decipher that Codex page.

"The wards—" Adelaide began.

"Are intact," Islington declared. "They always have been."

"Whatever you saw," Wilder said, keeping his focus on me, "has gone to ground."

"If you saw anything," Islington stated.

"I know what I saw," I seethed. "Did you see the gash on that kid's throat?"

"The alarms haven't sounded," Wilder said, cutting in before I got myself in even more trouble. "Which means it's still here."

I scoffed, "I think you mean it's still on the grounds since the *first time*."

"If it's a student who's come into contact with the

mutation, they'll have come back to maintain their cover," he went on. "For now, we take care of the injured and continue with our mission. We can't raise any suspicions until we flush them out."

"There has to be a way to detect them," I said. "The alarms…"

Adelaide shook her head. "We've already looked into this. Apart from putting wards on every doorway and window in the building, we don't have a way to test someone without their knowledge. We don't have the Light for the first option, or the technology for the second."

"So we have to go back to watching and waiting?" I complained. "Kayla's in the *infirmary*."

"We don't have any other option," Adelaide said. "Unless you can shed some light on the students, Scarlett."

"Do you know anyone who'd want to attack her?" Islington asked. "Since they're inviting you to their *illegal parties*, I assume you've gathered some actionable information."

"Everyone has it out for Kayla," I retorted. "She's the mean girl queen bee of this entire establishment. The whole student body wouldn't mind taking her down a peg or two."

"We don't encourage social hierarchy at this school," Islington stated. "We're training soldiers, not prom queens."

I rolled my eyes. Was he really that blind? "We really are scraping the bottom of the barrel."

His eyes narrowed in warning. "Excuse me?"

"You've got a lot more to worry about than a breach," I declared. "Your senior class is being terrorised by a bunch of bullies, one of which is now laying in the infirmary. If that's the best and brightest the Naturals have to offer, then we're screwed! We may as well lay down our arms right now."

"Is that your professional assessment, Miss Ravenwood?" Islington asked, his voice icy.

I squared my jaw. "One. Hundred. *Percent.*"

"Purples…" Wilder said, his voice low.

"I know you're low on recruits, Islington, but should we be looking into you?" I demanded. "You seem *out of touch.*"

"Enough!" he roared. "Your arrogance is becoming quite legendary, Miss Ravenwood. Don't let it be your downfall."

I scoffed. Speaking of downfalls, I wonder if he realised how much he was sheltering these kids' realities of life as a Natural. I knew I was older, and much less qualified, but even I knew the price this life asked of us. I just wasn't so sure the students did.

"Just because you've seen combat does not make you above reproach," Islington boomed. "You're still a student here, no matter your celebrity status, and will be treated as such. You smuggled a cold iron dagger into the Academy, and you endangered yourself and others through your reckless actions. You're bound to the immediate Academy grounds."

"*Seriously?*"

"Your movements will be tracked, you'll be assigned extra classes, and the moment you leave the boundary, *you're out of here.* I don't care about your mission, I won't have you undermine the authority of this Academy. *Do I make myself clear?*"

I slammed my fist down onto the desk. "But—"

"We're in his house, Purples," Wilder drawled. "You better listen to what he says."

Islington didn't take his cold stare off me. "Adelaide, if you would…"

The student councillor rose to her feet and gave me a sympathetic look as she raised her hands. Silver Light ebbed from her fingertips, growing into tendrils that wove around my body, infusing me with what I knew was a Natural tracking device.

They'd know where I was every moment of every day until it was removed. I didn't know if this was the dreaded detention everyone kept warning me about, but it still sucked. Being kept on a leash went against every fibre of my being.

When Adelaide was satisfied, she gave a curt nod in Islington's direction.

"Dismissed," the headmaster snapped.

Wilder grabbed my arm and dragged me from the office as if he sensed I was about to give Islington one last piece of my mind.

The door slammed closed, leaving Adelaide in there with the arsehat of the century. I began to walk away, the empty corridor throwing back the sound of my irritated footsteps. It had been a really great night until Kayla was attacked. Seriously, someone had to do something.

But how did it get in?

Trent had boasted about smuggling in the beer, which meant they had a way around the wards. I wasn't entirely sure about the alarms that detected any demonic presence, but either that Infernal had been hanging around the grounds for the past month, potentially jumping into everyone it came into contact with or someone had let it in.

The shite would hit the fan if I dobbed them in. I didn't want to say anything, not until I knew more. *What a mess.*

This year's senior class was lucky to have twenty students in it. If they all got expelled and implicated in this, then there'd be no new Naturals joining the fight for a long time. In a time where we needed every sword we could get, this was bad news.

"What?" Wilder asked, sensing my turmoil.

"Why do I always feel like I'm hitting my head against a brick wall?" I threw my hands into the air. "It's like they don't believe me."

"No one else saw it, but it doesn't mean it doesn't exist. I believe you, Purples."

"Then why does it feel like I'm fighting an uphill battle?"

"Bureaucracy is a bitch," he stated. "You know my stance on these things."

I cocked an eyebrow. "Buy now, pay later?"

"But don't get yourself into too much debt. Sometimes you're better off paying upfront than taking one of those deals."

"That's quite philosophical of you."

We walked down the hall, our banter seeming to

track towards the Scarlett and Wilder of old. Maybe it was because Greer was gone. I wondered if— No, I couldn't wonder about *that*.

"Do you think the arsehat back there is the thing I saw? He wasn't around until afterwards."

"Do you really want to ask him for an alibi?"

"Wouldn't hurt. It isn't like I can get into any more trouble."

"Islington isn't mutated," he said with a smirk. "As much as it would explain his behaviour, he's just a victim of his own arrogance."

"It takes one to know one, I guess." I rolled my eyes. "I'm not sure what's worse."

"Personal development is always a work in progress."

"Thanks for the dry assessment."

"You're welcome, Purples."

We approached the student dormitories and I felt Adelaide's tracking beacon—there was no other way to describe it—tingle. It felt like I was wearing an ankle bracelet. House arrest *indeed*.

"I feel like he's got it out for me."

Wilder lifted his eyebrows. "Who? Islington?"

I nodded.

"He doesn't like anyone challenging him. Back when we were training, he was an annoying twat, but now he's off the charts." He scratched at the stubble on his chin. "He's a stickler for the rules… If you want my advice, play his game."

The cogs in my brain began to turn. Buy now, pay later on an interest free plan that played to the

Academy's rules and regulations.

"Don't think too hard, Purples, otherwise your brain might explode."

"*Very funny.*"

I turned towards the door, then paused. "Keep an eye on Kayla," I added. "They might try again."

"Don't worry, Purples," Wilder said, pushing the door open for me, "no one will be getting close to that girl, believe me."

———

I shuffled into the kitchens the following morning, my head full of cobwebs. It wasn't just the lack of sleep that had me fuzzy, but the endless rush of thoughts I mulled over well into the small hours. I'd fallen asleep somewhere around the witching hour and woken with the sun.

Things were getting complicated around here—mysterious coins, shadow students, Infernals lurking on Academy grounds, and now I was lumped with magical GPS.

Tray in hand, I was looking for a quiet place to sit and nurse my grumpy morning mood when two out of the three mean girls blocked my path to serenity. Maisy and Trisha were in their full tactical gear, both bright-eyed for six-thirty a.m., especially considering the night they had before. I was seriously starting to miss my youth—skin elasticity included—and I was only twenty-five.

"You know it's weird you're at school when you're

old, right?" Maisy declared, glancing at my muesli. "It's not a good reflection on your upbringing."

"We shouldn't associate with people who've had a severe social disadvantage," Trisha added. "It takes years to become a full-fledged Natural, and you've only been around for, like, not even a year."

"And you're old," Maisy punctuated.

"Thanks for the reminder," I drawled, my hands tightening on my tray.

"So, what we're trying to say is, that if you want to eat lunch with us, you can sit at our table."

Trisha pried the tray out of my hands and set it down on the table. I guess I was eating my lunch with the cheerleaders today.

Sliding into the chair, I caught sight of Madeleine in the far corner, clearly disappointed with my new appointment. I shrugged and she turned her face away with a pout. I got it. She'd thought I'd sold out and all the advice I'd given her about things getting better was out the window.

Sighing, I picked up my spoon and stirred the muesli into the milk. The silverware clinked against the edges of the bowl as I glanced around the kitchen. There weren't many people in here, but it was Saturday morning.

"Where's Trent?" I asked, realising he wasn't here.

"He's still in the infirmary with Kayla." Trisha shrugged. "I guess he likes her or something."

"Oh, he totally likes her," Maisy stated.

"You're only just figuring it out?" I made a face. "Does Kayla like him?"

"He's too childish for her," Maisy said. "He acts like a ten-year-old."

"He's barely passing his classes," Trisha stated like it was a juicy piece of gossip.

Seriously, had these girls been at the same party I'd been at last night? They could go from a traumatic experience to gossip in one millisecond flat.

"You had all that beer last night," I began, testing the waters for some deep diving. "How do you get past the wards without triggering them?"

"Trent gets the stuff from a kid in the junior class," Maisy said with a shrug. "His older brother already graduated and passed on the secret. Why?"

"That demon got in somehow," I said.

The girls' faces began to turn white.

Maisy was the first one to string together a sentence. "Do you really think someone smuggled that thing in?"

"Why would someone do something like that?" Trisha wailed.

I really wish I could slap some sense into them, but instead, I sighed. Maybe this was the wake-up call they needed. A war was being fought, and soon they'd be out there fighting it. This wide-eyed crap would only get them killed or worse.

"Something's coming," I said, keeping my voice low. "Something big. We're all going to have to suck it up and do whatever we have to, to push back the demon incursion."

Both girls swallowed hard and glanced at one another. They understood what they were training for, but they'd never get the reality of it until they faced their first demon. The Academy protected them a little too much for my liking, but the war was reaching all the highly protected areas now. If the Darkness could breach the London Sanctum and make a play for the Codex, then they could get inside the Academy… and they had.

"There was a false alarm about a month ago," Trisha told me. "Right after classes started. But if something really got through, the teachers would've found it."

I nodded, wanting to keep them alert but not frightened. There was still some sense in being under the radar about a mutant shadow lurking on the grounds.

"They do have it under control," I said. "But it doesn't hurt to keep our eyes on it, too."

"It hurt Kayla," Maisy said. "We have to be ready if it happens again."

"That's the spirit!" I smiled, hoping I wouldn't get another strike for inciting violence.

"You went after Kayla last night like a proper Natural," Maisy said. "Weren't you scared?"

I shook my head. "There's a reason the Codex makes a big deal about not hesitating."

Trisha frowned, seeming to drop her cool girl façade. "Did you get into trouble? You had that dagger…"

I groaned dramatically and slumped back in my chair. "I'm Islington's enemy number one."

Maisy gasped and leaned across the table.

Grabbing my wrist, she yelped, "They put a tracker on you!"

"No way!" Trisha looked impressed, and I wondered if I'd just won another golden teenage ticket.

"It was stupid," I said. "I knew it might have been a demon, and all I had was a cold iron dagger. Without an arondight blade—"

"Andy said you saved Stewart Granger. His throat was all torn up."

"You guys went and got help and kept the others safe," I argued.

The girls glanced at one another.

"You've been out there," Maisy said, leaning across the table. "You've seen… *things*."

My brow furrowed. "*Yeah…*"

"Would you tell us about it?" Trisha asked, her cheeks flushing.

"Kayla always said they're not telling us enough and now she's in the infirmary," Maisy added.

"We're… Well, we're worried when we graduate and go out there that we'll choke."

What the…? They wanted me to be their Wilder to their Scarlett! How the tables had turned.

My lips curved into a smile. "I'll see what I can do."

The girls seemed to perk up at this and their shoulders straightened.

"Hey, we're going to see Kayla after breakfast," Trisha said. "Wanna come?"

I glanced at Madeleine, who was bent over her

cereal and a book across the room. "Maybe later. I've got detention-like things to do."

"Ugh," Trisha said with a pout. "They've put you on extra studies, haven't they?"

"Yeah, but that's cool." I shrugged. "I was doing twelve hours, seven days a week back at the Sanctum. This is a breeze compared to that."

"Seriously?" they exclaimed at the same time.

Thinking about all the training I'd done with Wilder, I felt a pang stab me directly in the heart. "I've got a lot of catching up to do."

"We have a training group this afternoon. Some the seniors get together to spar. You can come if you like?" Maisy offered. "Two o'clock, in the rear gym."

Man, if only this was ten years ago and it wasn't super demon hunter academy, imagine how much time I would've spent out of the principle's office. On second thought, nothing had changed at all. I was still rattling cages—only these cages were bigger and carried magical knives.

"Cool," I said. "Depends on what torture Islington's got me signed up for."

They spent the next five minutes consoling me before they decided to go see Kayla. Once they left, I scraped back my chair and stood. Dumping my tray with the kitchen staff, I ventured over to Madeleine.

Sensing I was standing in front of her, she raised her head and stared at me. She was doing her best anti-social 'you don't bother me' impersonation.

"Hey," I said.

"What?"

"Are you okay? I didn't see you last night."

She looked me over as I sat down, her expression changing. "I'm fine."

"There's a group of seniors training this afternoon. If I can get out of whatever extra classes Islington's lumped on me, you wanna go?"

"Like I'm invited to that," she scoffed. Gathering up her books, she pushed away from the table and stalked out of the kitchens, leaving me standing there like a lump.

I sighed and shook my head. I got it, I really did, but I was reaching out to Madeleine the best I could. If she really wanted to belong—even in her own irreverent way—it was up to her to reach back.

Problem was, I wasn't sure she wanted to.

12

———

I stopped by the infirmary before I headed to the library.

I hadn't been given a schedule for my extra detention classes yet, so I was taking advantage of my final minutes as a somewhat free woman.

Lingering outside, I peered through the windows of the infirmary. It was a similar setup as the London Sanctum—rows of beds with white curtains between each, tables and medical equipment scattered here and there, and a skeleton staff. It seemed like some faculty rotated in and out between teaching, covering the places where they were spread too thin.

The historical aspect of the Academy had even spread here, and I was surprised to see it looked more like a World War II-esque trauma centre than a school sick bay. Hints of modern technology were amongst the antique decor, only adding to the mystery of the queer alternate future world of the Naturals.

Kayla was propped up in bed towards the back, the covers pulled up around her waist. She was wearing bright pink pyjamas and her hair was loose and wild as she chatted excitedly to Trisha and Maisy—likely telling them everything that'd happened last night.

I spotted Trent as he pushed out into the hall, his eyes rimmed with dark circles. It looked like he'd been up all night.

"How is she?" I asked, noticing he was wearing the same clothes he'd worn to the party. "She seems okay."

"She's going to be fine," he replied, stifling a yawn. "But she doesn't remember what happened to her or how she ended up in the forest."

"I suppose that's to be expected. It looked like she hit her head pretty hard. What did they say happened to her?"

"She was hit by something," Trent explained. "It knocked her out cold, but I heard them whisper about traces of Darkness."

I frowned, thinking back to the shadow creature. The Infernal had said that thing had attacked Kayla. Had the demon stopped it from doing something worse? It seemed the likely conclusion as they'd been arguing about maintaining their cover.

"She's lucky," I said. "We must have startled it."

We stood in the hall, the silence of the empty Academy heavy around us. Trent threw me a look and scuffed his boot against the polished concrete floor. What was with the eighteen-hundreds and terrazzo?

"You can say anything to me, you know," I stated. "I'm not in league with 'The Man'." I air quoted.

"I can't believe that kid was possessed," he blurted, shaking his head in disbelief. "Stewart Granger. He was, like, only fourteen and that demon possessed him. They took him away this morning and no one will say where he went."

I knew he'd been taken to the London Sanctum where Ramona would test for mutation. He'd be safe with her and Jackson. Hopefully, he hadn't been infected but if he had, maybe it wasn't too late to reverse the effects completely. Only time would tell.

"You know what can happen when someone is possessed by an Infernal," I said.

"Yeah. He could get soul sick."

I patted him on the shoulder. "I'm sure they've taken him to one of the Sanctums. They can monitor him better there. They don't like to say too much about these things for safety reasons."

"I know. It's just…"

"I get it," I said, attempting to be reassuring about all the secrecy. "When I first showed up, it annoyed the hell outta me, too. I like to know what's going on. I still don't half the time."

"But you seemed so calm."

I shrugged. "I've been out there, I suppose. Being purple has its drawbacks."

"I thought you had it easier… you know, being touched by Arondight and all."

"I thought so, too," I drawled. "But it doesn't make me any more special than any other Natural. I should've waited for the teachers."

"But you saved Stewart," he argued.

I sighed, conflicted on what stance I should be taking. One of these days I'd run headfirst into danger and not be so lucky.

"Trent…" I turned and looked him over with a frown, "how did you get that beer?"

"I, uh…" He trailed off, looking sheepish.

"I'm not going to dob on you," I murmured. "I'm just trying to help. Ever since I found out who I really was, demon activity has been on the rise. They think we're one step away from finding Arondight, and they'll do anything to stop us."

"Is that why a demon was on the grounds?"

"If there's a way through the wards, you have to tell someone," I murmured. "Kayla could've been possessed or worse."

"Did I do this to her?" he asked, his eyes widening. "Did I let it in?"

"I don't think so, but if there's a vulnerability in the wards, it might happen again." I gave him a stern look. "Do you understand?"

He nodded, looking back at Kayla. It was still open for debate if he was going to follow through and tell someone about the smuggling operation the students had going on. I just hoped he made the right decision.

These kids were going to have to grow up fast if they were going to make it.

As I walked through the Academy towards the library, I realised just how much I was missing the chaos of the London Sanctum.

It wasn't just Jackson's absence that had me down, but Romy, Valeria, Alo, and even Martin's. At this mashed-up manor house in the Cotswolds, I felt as if I was wedged between two worlds and this time, it wasn't the human and the supernatural. It was the teenagers and the grown-ups.

Hopefully, Aiden had some good news because I was becoming a junkie looking for her next hit of the good stuff.

I fist-bumped Galahad's suit of armour as I walked past—well, as close as the glass cabinet would allow me—and made my way through the warren of books, artifacts, and curious students to the office at the back.

I nudged open the door with my boot and leaned against the jamb. Aiden was buried under his usual pile of books and papers, his glasses halfway down his nose. He really needed to get those things tightened.

To my surprise, Madeleine was sitting in the opposite chair with an open book in her lap.

"Fancy seeing you here," I declared.

"Scarlett," Aiden said smiling.

"Hey, Madeleine."

She glared at me and rose to her feet. "Thanks," she said to Aiden, "I'll see you Wednesday."

Gathering her books, she smiled at him before

whirlwinding from the room. I stepped to the side, narrowly avoiding a strategically placed shoulder.

"She thinks I've sold out," I said, glancing over my shoulder. She must get extra tutoring. I didn't even know that was something Aiden did outside of hiding in his office. "You tutor her?"

"Twice a week. She's a good student," Aiden remarked. "She's got great aptitude, but she's unhappy."

"She doesn't fit in at the Academy, but she'll find her place once she graduates."

"You sound like you're speaking from experience."

I smirked. "I am."

He leaned back in his chair. "It's good to see you in one piece, by the way."

"I've got a knack for getting into trouble."

"You're getting quite the reputation for it, though I'm sure those students are glad you were around."

"Tell that to Islington," I complained, sitting on the chair next to the overflowing desk. "He's put me under house arrest."

"Well, technically you are a student."

"Thanks for the reminder."

Aiden chuckled and patted me on the arm. "Don't worry about Liam. He's not too bad under all the stiff upper lip."

A laugh escaped me and I began to relax. Islington really did have a stick up his arse.

"We had a scare, but everyone's going to be fine," Aiden went on. "I hear your friend Wilder is out looking for evidence."

My laughter faded. "He is?"

"Something about figuring out how the Infernal could hide on the grounds for so long. The alarms went off over a month ago. That's a long time to lurk without anyone noticing."

I tensed, realising Aiden didn't know anything about the mutations. Perhaps I should keep it that way… for now.

"I can see that look in your eye." He shook a finger at me. "My brother gets it when he talks about fighting demons. You want to be out there helping with the search, but I promise, you'll want to be in here when you hear what I've found out about your coin."

"You have?" My focus shifted and my eyes widened. This was the hit of good news I was hoping for. *C'mon, bang of serotonin.*

Aiden chuckled and opened the desk drawer. Retrieving a plastic baggie, he opened the snap-lock and gave me back the coin.

"It's not a bale seal," he said. "It's proof of *membership*."

"Membership? To what?" Remembering Greer's theory about a secret society that protected Arondight, my ears pricked up.

"*Ordo Enim Geminae Flammae*," he said. "It's Latin for the Order of the Twin Flames."

Twin flames? "*Arondight and Excalibur.*"

Aiden nodded. "Arondight is called the Indigo Flame, and before Excalibur was broken, it was known as the Argent Flame."

"What's argent?"

"Argent is the tincture of silver," he explained. "Humanity and Naturals were obsessed with heraldry and status back then. It was all knights and chivalry and power through bloodlines. Tinctures were a way to define the limited colours and patterns used in various coat of arms. It was a massive faux pas to mistake one family for another."

I snorted and turned the coin over in my palm. "So basically, it's just a posh way of saying silver."

"*Exactly.*"

"So this Order… They probably knew where Arondight was."

Aiden clicked his fingers. "Which means we have to find them."

I turned the coin over in my hand, studying the worn surface. He was one step away from becoming the Natural version of Indiana Jones, but I wasn't so quick to leap when there were still so many unknowns.

The puzzle piece seemed to fit with my memories of my parents. Why no one knew them, why Markzoth had been hunting them, why hiding me had been so important. They'd laid down their lives to protect me because even then, I'd held a piece of Arondight inside me.

Still, it seemed so fantastical. My parents were part of the Order of the Twin Flames—tasked with protecting the whereabouts of Arondight and maybe even the recovery of Excalibur. Markzoth knew it, the druidess knew it—and they were both waiting for me to resurface. Something had been put into motion the night Wilder and I met, but what? The End of Times?

I ran my fingers over my scar and despite myself, I felt my Light simmer underneath the surface.

If the Order was still around, wouldn't they have found me by now? I'd well and truly made myself known by killing greater demons and uncovering the Inquisitor's betrayal, but what if the Order died with my parents? That could mean I was the world's last hope. Arondight was gone, and I was the only thing standing between humanity and total annihilation.

It seemed as if the rediscovery of the lost sword was inevitable. Either that, or there was an incoming plot twist.

"There has to be a reason I found this," I whispered.

"It's definitely not a coincidence," Aiden said. "There's a clue we're missing though, and I can't quite put my finger on it."

What if I needed this to access something? Like a hidden cache, or a secret meeting chamber, or the actual place where Arondight was hidden? When the Codex showed me the sword, it was hidden behind a shimmering veil of water.

I held up the coin and started at the symbol. The twisting flame that was the heraldry of the Order of the Twin Flames. There was only one other place it'd shown up.

"The stone circle," I exclaimed. "The page from the Codex…"

"Did you talk to Greer before she left?"

My excitement started to fade and I shook my head. I was good at confrontation when it was a possessed corpse, but now that I knew her and Wilder were a thing just made everything ache. Unrequited love sucked. *Big time*. The next time I see Jackson, I have to apologise… again.

Aiden coughed nervously. "I can put in a call—"

"*No*," I interrupted. "I mean, can we just keep this to ourselves? The fewer people who know, the better."

Aiden raised his eyebrows. "Do you have a way to decipher the code? Because I sure don't."

I shook my head.

"Codes like this aren't just about finding the cypher," he went on. "There's Light involved, which makes this inherently more difficult."

"I'm used to uphill battles," I said.

"Scarlett…"

I looked up. "What?"

"Just be careful, okay?" He frowned, his gaze falling to my hand. "You're the key to everything, you do realise that, right?"

"Yeah, I know. I kinda wish everyone would stop reminding me, though."

"I'm starting to wonder if all the reminders are necessary considering your taste for adrenaline."

I laughed, mainly because it was the only thing left to do. I'd had my heart broken, I was in the middle of a conspiracy, I may or may not be the key to ending or saving the world, and I was a twenty-five-year-old high school student with one hell of an epic detention.

I was officially in over my head.

All I knew was that I couldn't do it alone anymore. Only one person had been there from the beginning, and he might be reluctant and surly, but right now, he was all I had outside of this library.

It was time to tell Wilder the truth.

"Thanks, Aiden, but I've gotta go." I pocketed the coin and made for the door.

"Where are you going?" he called out after me.

Turning, I flashed him a smile. "I've got to do a few things before I'm put on full lockdown."

"Like what?" He narrowed his eyes and put on his teacher face.

"Don't worry, I'm not going to break the honour code." I crossed my fingers in a silent pledge.

Aiden grimaced and pushed his glasses back into place. "Why do I get the feeling I'm better off not knowing?"

13

———

I wandered through the Academy, opening my senses.

Searching for Wilder used to be so easy, but I'd closed myself off from him for so long and now it was like I'd forgotten how. Maybe it was a subconscious thing. I didn't want to face the truth of his lack of feelings for me, so I was unconsciously protecting myself.

If only it were that easy.

He didn't know I'd overheard and saw them the other night. I could pretend I was still ignorant, right?

Right?

Ever since I'd syphoned his power at the Necropolis, I seemed to know where he was. All I had to do was open myself to him, which had been a huge problem. I'd kept that book closed for obvious reasons, and now I need it and it wasn't working.

If I couldn't find him, I knew he'd be hiding some place high up. Rooftops were his favourite.

I'd wandered for what felt like hours before I finally felt the familiar tingle in the back of my mind. He was close… and always had been.

Ironically, I found him perched above the library. I had to go through a dark hallway and a dusty attic to find the trap door, but his Light was like a beacon to me now.

I moved though the hatch, closing it softly behind me. A walkway wove around the interior of the roof, the border marked with wrought iron spikes. I didn't know why people would come up here, but it was a feature of most of these old manor houses.

Wilder had gone beyond the safety of the walkway and had moved out onto the tiles so he could dangle his boots over the edge.

"Took you long enough," he said.

I grunted and sat next to him, kicking my feet in the air beside his.

"I thought I would've seen you up here long before now, but I suppose we both know why."

"You're still butt-hurt about that?"

"I've seen the way the librarian looks at you," he drawled. "You're a real nerd magnet, you know that?"

"*Shut up*."

"Are the insults out of your system now?"

"Are they out of yours?"

We eyed one another in the ultimate staring competition. A full minute passed, and just when my eyes were about to water, Wilder blinked, and the trance was broken.

"Did you hear about Brax?" he asked.

"Huh?" I'd been so wrapped up in my own little world that I'd forgotten about the drama with the Regula.

"Wainthrope was sentenced today. That's why Greer left so abruptly."

"I hope he got what was coming to him," I drawled.

"He did. His Light was stripped, and he was bound to the catacombs under Glastonbury."

"Glastonbury?" I made a face. "I hope his cell is directly underneath a mosh pit full of gumboot-wearing hippies."

Wilder snorted.

"What's that about Brax?"

"He's been appointed the temporary Inquisitor."

"*Ugh.*" It couldn't happen to a better person. All the authority figures in this world were so surly it gave me a headache. "He's one of us. Maybe it won't be so bad."

Wilder grimaced and looked back out across the Cotswolds.

"What?" I prodded. I didn't like when he got that look on his face—it only meant trouble.

"I always wondered why he wasn't there that night."

"Who?"

"Brax. He wasn't there when we went back to the Sanctum to take on Wainthrope."

"He's on the council, I'm sure he was just trying to protect himself from being captured. We just got there first."

Wilder shrugged. "Maybe."

I could tell it bothered him, but I didn't know what else to say, so I let the conversation fall into a lull. Now, how did I start the story about how I accidentally killed the last Druid, the funky coin she gave me, and the supposed secret society my parents were a part of? Did I open with a hearty *once upon a time*?

But Wilder saved me from myself.

"I've got something for you." He reached inside his jacket and pulled out a familiar plastic toy.

I stared at the troll doll and a weird feeling flowed through me. I thought I'd never see it again.

"Where'd you get that?" I asked knowing full well how he'd come by it.

"I nicked it off Greer," he replied. "She had it in her room and neglected to return it."

I snatched it from him and held it close. It felt tainted now, knowing it'd been in the room when they'd... *ahem*... but at least she didn't have it anymore.

"Things are frosty with you two," he said, watching me carefully.

"I guess." I closed my hand around the troll's hair and smoothed it up into a point.

"Am I risking my life if I ask you why?"

I had the feeling he already knew why, but I wasn't at the stage where I was comfortable bringing it up with him. They'd been talking about my feelings as if they were an annoyance. *She has feelings for you...* Right after that part, Wilder had kissed Greer.

"You're right," I murmured, my heart aching. "Something happened to me at the Necropolis."

"I hope this is the part where you tell me about it."

My shoulders sank. "When I used my piece of Arondight, I was… open… to everything. Then I was gone."

"Gone?"

I nodded. "Someone called me back."

"Who?"

"I don't know. I barely remember it. So much has been going on, I forgot about it. After that, everything seems so much more…" I was having trouble finding the words to describe just how adrift I felt in the complexity of what I held inside me. "I didn't understand it, not until now."

"That's why you're supposed to talk about things," Wilder said. "Things might be complicated, but you can trust me."

I was beginning to wish he'd never kissed me. That's when it all started to go downhill. If he was just surly Wilder and I was just annoying Scarlett, then everything would be fine.

I took the coin out of my pocket and squeezed my fist around it. So much had happened since the Necropolis. How did I tell him about it?

"Here." I slid the coin into his palm, my heart leaping as my hand fit against his.

"A coin?" He turned it over, studying the worn symbols.

"The druidess gave it to me when I went back for Jackson," I said.

"Is this what you've been hiding?" He gave me a look, then went back to studying the silver disc.

"She foresaw her death," I murmured. "She saw me return. Everything she made us do—keeping Jackson as collateral, going after the runes… It was all just an elaborate scheme to get me to go back alone."

"Then that coin and the words she gave you were more important to the world than prolonging her life. She lived that long in hiding to give that to you, Purples."

I looked at him, the gravity of what he said too fantastical to comprehend.

"Think about it," he said.

Had the druidess been in hiding for hundreds of years, prolonging her life, on the hope that her vision was true? If so, she'd been waiting for me all that time. *Me*, a smart-mouthed, purple-haired orphan with a penchant for danger.

"*The future is unwritten,*" I said, echoing the druidess' prophetic words, "*but the past holds all the secrets. All the power. Past losses, reborn futures.*"

"The past holds all the secrets…" Wilder mused. "Past losses. Reborn futures? Is that what she told you?"

I nodded. It sounded like a crazy prophecy and I wasn't sure I believed in those. "I wish I understood what it means."

"Any number of things, I guess," Wilder said with a grunt. "What do you know about the coin?"

"Aiden's been helping me figure out what the symbols mean."

"*Purples.*"

"Don't worry, I trust him," I argued. "I wouldn't know anything if it wasn't for him. I only gave him the coin, I never told him about the druidess or what she had said. Somehow, I thought I should keep that to myself."

Wilder closed his fist around the coin and shook his head. "I hope he found something useful."

"*Ordo Enim Geminae Flammae*," I declared.

"The Order of the Twin Flames?" Of course, Wilder was fluent in Latin. He was such a know-it-all sometimes, it made me want to puke.

"I think my parents were part of it," I murmured. "I think they were keeping me hidden because of the piece of Arondight inside me. I think they were trying to recover Excalibur, too."

Wilder snorted. "That's a lot of thinking."

"Questions," I mused. "That's all the answers I've found. No full stops, just more question marks."

"Maybe they found a piece and the only way to keep it safe—"

"Was to put it inside me."

"No one would think to look for a piece of sword inside a kid," he mused. "Even now, no one suspects it. They all think you simply touched it."

"If they only had a piece, then they probably never found the rest of it." I turned the troll doll around so its face was peering across the landscape.

"The druidess gave you that coin for a reason, Purples," Wilder said. "Did she say anything else?"

I shook my head. "I think they're all gone now."

"Who? This Order?"

"Yeah. I mean, wouldn't they have contacted me by now? If my parents were the last, then no wonder they put the, whatever you want to call it, inside me."

"Don't say that," Wilder said with a frown. "All this is just speculation."

"It's the only thing that makes sense, and trust me, nothing has made much of it since I met you."

"It's my pleasure," he drawled.

"That flame symbol on the back, Aiden found it in the Codex."

"The Codex?" Wilder turned over the coin and studied the image. "What did the page say?"

"Nothing we could decipher. It was written in code."

Wilder opened his mouth but closed it just as quickly. I knew what he was going to say. 'Get Greer to consult the real Codex.'

We fell into an uneasy silence, the night stretching before us. In the distance, I could just make out the curve of the hills around the Academy, the rises hiding the valleys the Cotswolds were famous for.

I'd missed this. Just sitting some place high with Wilder, simply watching the world pass below. It was a strange feeling, missing the thing that hurt me the most.

"Sometimes I wonder if I'm going to survive this," I said, staring out over the rolling hills.

"Of course you are," Wilder stated matter-of-factly. "If anyone is going to come out the other side of this war, it's you, Purples."

"How can you be so sure?"

"Have you met yourself?"

"On a daily basis."

Wilder's lips quirked and I couldn't help but smile back.

"I still stand by what I said. You remind me of me when I was at the Academy," he leaned closer, "brilliant and insubordinate."

"I'm not quite sure if you're complimenting me or trying to inflict a mortal wound on my self-confidence."

"I'm complimenting you, Scarlett." *Uh oh, he was using my full name again.*

"Put this one on the back burner, teach," I grunted and took the coin off him. "We've got more pressing problems right now. There's a shadow creature that may or may not be a mutated student hiding somewhere inside this Academy."

"I believe you saw it, Purples, but I haven't been able to find a trace."

"I heard you'd been out and about today."

"Jealous?"

"Kind of. I miss my arondight blade."

He smiled and shook his head. "It hasn't left anything behind. There were hints of Darkness on Kayla, but it didn't lead anywhere. The grounds were clean, and the wards are airtight."

Maybe not completely airtight, but I was still

holding out that Trent would suck it up and tell someone about how they got the beer through. If he didn't come clean soon, then I would.

"There's one student I've been keeping my eye on," he said. "I think you know him."

"Who?"

"Trent O'Connor."

"Trent?" I asked, my eyebrows rising. "*No way.* Uh-ah."

"Think about it, Purples. He's been around every single time something's happened, and his behaviour is becoming more and more erratic."

"It's not him. He was in the clearing when Kayla was attacked. I saw him. I was talking to him."

"Maybe so, but I think he knows something."

"And you want me to grill him?" I sighed. That kid was going to be the death of me.

"It isn't like the students are confiding their secrets to me," Wilder drawled. "You're one of the cool kids, Purples. You get invited to all the parties and sit with the cliques at lunch."

"It was *one* party," I complained. "It's not like I'm buying into the do-over."

He laughed and knocked his shoulder against mine. "Just keep an eye on him. We're up against it and time is not on our side."

He didn't have to remind me. Every day things were tipping closer towards Darkness, and Arondight was still out of reach. To make matters worse, the Naturals seemed to be falling apart and their new generation was severely under prepared.

"These kids are under so much pressure," I murmured. "And they're too sheltered."

"It wasn't like this when I was here," Wilder confided. "Islington's made them soft."

"They told me they haven't even seen a demon before. They came to me and asked if I could help them prepare," I scoffed and rubbed my eyes. "They asked *me*. Can you see the irony?"

Wilder scowled and curled his hands into tight fists. "No matter what, things are going to change around here. I'll make sure of it."

14

────────

"**S**carlett Ravenwood."

My eyes snapped open and I stared up into a red-faced Masters. He was glowering at me, his displeasure apparent. It wasn't the first time I'd fallen asleep during guided meditation, but this time, I hadn't been able to quiet my mind.

Two days after the party, things had begun to settle, even though there was a renewed heaviness in the air. Monday morning classes resumed as normal, and Kayla had been released from the infirmary with her report saying she'd received nothing more than a concussion.

For what it was worth, the students believed the Infernal was killed and the threat was over, but I knew better.

"Sorry," I squeaked.

"Pay attention, Miss Ravenwood," Masters barked. "Remind me and the class why we meditate."

I pouted. Wilder had never made me sit cross-legged on the floor so I could clear my mind. His idea of centering oneself was violence and snarky teachable moments. I couldn't get a handle on all this.

"Meditation increases stress resilience," I said.

"And?"

"Allows us to focus our Light."

"Why?"

I squirmed. "So we don't lose control."

"And it doesn't help if we fall asleep in the middle of it," he stated, causing the class to snigger. "*Quiet!*" He turned back to me with a glare. "Since you're on probation, I want you to keep a meditation diary."

"A diary?" I moaned.

"Yes, Miss Ravenwood, *a diary*. One hour every morning and evening, and I expect you to sign off with your Light so I know you're not cheating." He eyed me with a smug satisfaction. "Understood?"

I made a face and nodded. "Yes, sir."

He checked his watch, then waved at the class. "That's all for today. Don't forget your studies. Remember to always be vigilant."

The class erupted into a clamour of movement as they gathered their things and marched from the room. I slumped my shoulders and followed suit, wondering when I was going to get my schedule of torture. It must be something pretty damn sadistic if Islington hadn't finished compiling it yet.

"Miss Ravenwood?"

I rolled my eyes at the sound of Masters' voice, feeling like I was sixteen again. Turning, I hung back to see what he wanted.

"Here's your revised schedule." He thrust a piece of paper at me. "If you ask me, you got lucky."

I nodded, sensing it was a good idea not to poke at the faculty any more than I already had. Threatening the headmaster was already well over the line, but enraging Masters might give the poor man a heart attack.

"If it wasn't for your quick thinking, Stewart might not be with us today," he went on. "I can't say I approve of the way you went about it, but…" he trailed off with a shrug.

I stared at him in shock, barely believing what I was hearing. Masters was complimenting me?

"You don't need this school, Miss Ravenwood," he said, waving the schedule at me. "But you do need control. Please take the time to listen, because we teach everything for a reason."

I took the paper from his hand and swallowed the lump in my throat. Somehow hearing those words come out of his mouth had me all choked up.

"Go on," he said, nodding towards the door, "you don't want to be late for your next class."

"Thank you," I muttered as I backed away.

Masters smiled—though it looked more like a twisted grimace—and shooed me out of the room as the next wave of students began to file in.

Outside, I wandered down the hall, catching up with the pack of seniors heading towards the gym.

"I don't remember how I got there," Kayla was saying. "One second I was in the clearing by the bonfire, then I was in the forest."

Oh great, she was giving a rendition of her brush with death like it was a scripted scene on a reality TV show.

"Did you see who attacked you?" one of the boys asked.

"It all happened so fast," she said with a flourish. "One moment I was standing there, the next, I was on the ground. It all happened so fast."

Typical Kayla. She loved being the centre of attention, especially since she had such an enraptured audience. I wondered if she'd still be boasting if she knew what actually had attacked her.

"You were lucky," Maisy said. "That Infernal could've hurt you way worse."

"Poor Stewart," Kayla cried.

"I heard they took him to London," one of the girls stated.

I snorted and looked at my new schedule and was surprised to see junior demonology had morphed into senior combat training. In fact, the word junior was nowhere to be seen. I wasn't sure if this was a promotion but moving from one-on-one to a group class was a step in the right direction. Maybe this was how I could help these kids prepare for the real world.

What was it Wilder said to me after the showdown in Islington's office? *Buy now, pay later?*

I crumpled the schedule in my hand, narrowed my eyes, and followed the others to the gym. All my favourite people from Light studies were there—Kayla, Maisy and Trisha, Trent, Andy, Rhiannon, Fiona, Grant, Max, and Madeleine.

"Hey, Scarlett's in our class now," Trisha said, perking up as I joined the girls in the locker room.

"It seems like Islington's got a sense of humour," I drawled. Or maybe he'd actually listened to my rant in his office.

"This is great," Trisha said.

"Finally," Kayla said as she changed into her stock standard black Natural active wear. "We'll get to see the infamous Natural touched by Arondight in action."

Madeleine emerged from a cubicle where she'd locked herself in so she could change away from the others. The door collided with the wall, causing everyone to stare.

"What?" she spat, rolling her eyes.

The girls looked at one another and burst into laughter as the goth girl strode out of the locker room.

"What's that all about?" I asked, casting out my imaginary fishing line.

"Madeleine's a freak," one of the girls said.

"Yeah," Kayla declared, "she's always so moody and weird. She wears all that black makeup and never talks to anyone."

I snorted and shook my head. "Just because she's different, doesn't make her any less of a Natural. You should be sticking together."

"Unlikely," Kayla drawled. "Madeleine thinks she's better than everyone else. She needs some cutting down to size."

The other girls laughed as their leader walked out into the gym. That was her royal decree, I supposed.

Madeleine closed down and threw herself into her studies to make herself less of a target, but the others only saw it as her acting superior. The poor girl was in a lose-lose situation.

Glancing after Kayla, I wasn't sure what to call my punishment anymore. Detention? Probation? Torture? It felt like a combination of all three. Extra classes, extra homework, extra hassle, extra Kayla drama.

Sighing, I stashed my bag in the lockers and went out to join the rest of the class, but when I saw who the teacher was, I began to wonder what I'd done to anger the universe. Gone were the days of private training with Patrick and here I was, stewing in my own self-inflicted sexual tension.

Wilder smirked at me and nodded towards the mat. "Nice of you to join us."

I groaned and shoved past him.

"You did this, didn't you?" I hissed.

"You said it yourself, Purples. They came to you for help. This is how we help them."

"By breaking even more Academy rules?"

His lips quirked. "Aw, you know me so well."

I made a face and lined up with the rest of the students, but Wilder had other ideas.

"Scarlett, choose your weapon."

"Huh?"

"Everyone wants to see what you can do, so let's show them."

I glanced at the others.

"Go on, Scarlett," Maisy coaxed.

"You've fought demons before," Trisha added. "We want to see you up against Mr. Wilder."

"Mr. Wilder?" I shot him a look.

"The first rule of sparing is to respect your teachers," he stated. "Don't dilly dally, Miss Ravenwood."

Dilly dally? Since when did Wilder use words like that?

I snorted and approached the rack of practice weapons against the wall, my bare feet padding across the cold mat.

There were various things to choose from, like wooden swords, staffs, and daggers. I'd fought with them all, but I'd always liked the staff the best. Nothing could beat an arondight blade out in the field, but in here, the staff was my go-to.

I picked up my weapon of choice and turned to face Wilder.

"Good choice," he said, taking the second staff. "The long reach compensates for your stubby arms."

The students began to laugh, and I narrowed my eyes as I assumed the position at one end of the mat.

"You know the rules," Wilder began. "A strike is a point. First to ten, or yield, ends the bout. If you use your Light, you forfeit."

"I hope you know what you're doing," I said as we began to circle one anther.

"I always know what I'm doing."

While he was busy smirking, I lunged, feigning left, then weaving right. I tapped him on the hip as he blocked the wrong strike.

"Pay attention, *Mr. Wilder.*"

He attacked, striking hard and fast. I met each blow with my staff, twisting and ducking, then returning fire. I cried out as I swung, trying to keep my emotions in check. I was dying to put him on his arse, but he'd taught me that desperation was a surefire way to wind up on mine instead.

Wilder rapped me on the leg, then I clipped his arm. He swung, I ducked, he leaped, I twisted. It was like old times and before long, we'd fallen back into the easy rhythm we had when we trained at the London Sanctum.

In the end, Wilder had to call time because we weren't getting anywhere. He was either my match, or he'd taught me so well that I could anticipate his moves… because they were the ones he'd make.

Maybe now the rest of the students might take me more seriously—as if facing off with an Infernal with nothing more than a cold iron dagger wasn't enough.

For the rest of the class, we were put through a series of drills that had everyone pushing up against a wall. Dripping with sweat, Wilder didn't let us off. If anything, this workout was more stressful than the ones he put me through at the Sanctum. I guess he really meant it when he said things were going to change.

By the time we'd hit the showers, if someone wasn't in a bad mood, they were about to drop. Thank goodness it was lunchtime because we were all a little hangry—so hungry we were angry.

I was sitting on a bench outside the locker rooms

lacing my boots when Kayla made a face at me. Everyone was on their way to get prime position in the lineup for crumbed chicken Monday. I couldn't blame them—it was good chicken.

"What?" I asked, bracing myself for a blast of 'teenage girl'.

"Are student-teacher relations a thing if you're a geriatric?" she declared in her best snooty voice.

"Next time I run towards danger to save your life, remind me of this moment," I replied, turning my attention to Trent. He was skulking across the gym, watching the other boys.

She gasped dramatically. "You didn't just say that!"

The female obsession over handsome, damaged brawn in this place was infuriating. "Don't bite the hand that feeds you, Kayla."

She flicked her hair over her shoulder and stalked off, taking the others with her. Trisha was tugging at her sleeve, trying to talk sense into her, but she was just slamming her head into a brick wall.

I lingered, my gaze sliding to Trent, who'd just ducked into the boys' locker room with a dodgy look on his face. Wilder was right about something at least. Trent was up to something.

Taking advantage of the empty gym, I crossed the mats and barged past the boy sign that forbade girls from entering.

To my shock, it wasn't the stinky urinals that made me recoil. Trent was leaning over the counter, *snorting lines*.

"What is this?" I demanded, stalking across the bathroom. "You're doing drugs?"

He let out a yelp. "Just a little. I—"

"*Trent.*"

"It's not like that!"

I snatched the baggie that was sitting in front of the mirror and began to dump the contents into the sink.

"Scarlett!"

"If it's not like that, then explain it to me," I demanded, turning on the tap. Water rushed out, swirling around and around, sucking the powder down the plughole.

"I just need a little extra energy, that's all," he wailed. "*I promise.*"

"Don't lie to me, Trent," I snapped. "I've heard it all before, you know. Growing up, I wasn't one of the cool kids. I was always getting into trouble and hanging around the wrong crowd, so believe me when I say I've heard these excuses before."

"*Scarlett…*" He fisted his hands into his hair.

"You need to get it together," I said. "If you're struggling, you can ask for help. You don't have to go through it alone."

"I can't. They'll kick me out and… If I can't keep up, they'll expel me."

"There are better ways of going about it than snorting some weird arse magical Natural drug." Reaching out, I slapped him on the back of the head.

"Ow!"

"You do realise you'll get expelled over this, right?"

"You can't tell anyone," he wailed.

Oh, for heaven's sake… I was trapped in the ultimate supernatural teen movie.

Trent began to pace, his anxiety rising with each lap.

"Talk to me," I told him. "I'm here and I'm listening."

He blinked, but his mouth remained closed.

"I took the rap for you with Masters, remember? You owe me one."

He came to a standstill, obviously torn as to what to say. I caught him, so he had to tell me something, but if it was the truth or a lie to get himself out of trouble was another thing entirely.

"I…" He took a deep breath. "After seeing how you went after the thing that attacked Kayla, I knew I'd never make it. I choked, Scarlett. I'm barely passing my classes and… I couldn't protect her."

"If you focused more on training and less on impressing girls and looking cool, you'd pass as one of the top seniors," I stated. "*Fact.*"

"You really think so?" The hope in his eyes broke my purple heart.

"There's too few of us, Trent. I know it's a big deal, but we're dedicating our lives to stopping an apocalypse. No one can shoulder that alone. We're here to help one another, but if you need to cheat to pass training, then you're just buying yourself a one-way ticket to an early grave."

He ran his hands over his face and cursed. "I've really screwed up, haven't I?"

"No," I murmured grasping his shoulders. "You've got your whole life ahead of you. It's not too late to knuckle down and get your grades back up."

"I don't know how."

I let him go and bit my bottom lip. Trent was a good kid, he just needed some guidance and someone who wouldn't take any shite when he slipped. He needed someone like...*Wilder*.

"You can go to Wilder," I said, hoping I was doing the right thing. We were on rocky ground, but that didn't mean my onetime mentor wouldn't help. After all, Greer said he was a changed man.

"Mr. Wilder?" Trent starred at me. "But that guy's so mean."

"No, he's *surly*, there's a difference." I shook my head. "You can trust him. I'll have a word, okay?"

He nodded and looked at the sink.

"We'll help you get back on track, but you have to promise me one thing," I said.

"*Anything*."

"No more drugs, okay?"

He nodded furiously and wiped at his eyes.

"Take a beat before your next class, okay?"

"Thanks, Scarlett."

Sighing, I walked out of the boys' locker room, realising I was going to miss lunch. Way to go keeping on time for my first day of punishment. My stomach was going to complain until dinnertime. I wondered if

I was going to get demerit points for disrupting other students with all the gurgling.

Rounding the corner, I almost smacked into Wilder. My heart leapt into my throat and I cursed the way I wished that if I had kept going, I'd be in his arms right now. *Moron.*

"Don't do that!" I exclaimed, giving him the dirtiest look I could muster. It wasn't hard, all things considered.

He crossed his arms over his chest and raised his eyebrows. "Well?"

"Well what?"

"I saw you slink into the men's room. Did it live up to your expectations? Were the urinal cakes well stocked?"

"You're clutching at straws," I replied, ignoring his baiting. "Seeing things where there isn't any."

"Like?"

"Do you think this place is getting to you more than you'd like to admit?"

Wilder eyed me and shrugged. "I know how to leave the past behind, do you?"

"That's not what this is about."

"Then what is it about, if it isn't about *that*?"

I glared at him, annoyed at his over-achieving skill for saying everything without actually saying the words outright. He was with Greer now and anything that happened with us, including that one time he kissed me, was on the way to going exactly where he implied it should be. Still, I wouldn't give him the satisfaction.

"Trent's a teenage boy dealing with teenage boy things," I hissed at him. "Except with the pressure of life and death on his shoulders."

"It's been done this way for a thousand years, Purples."

I raised my eyebrows. "Failure isn't an option. Do you understand how that can screw with a kid who's barely passing their classes? Not everyone is like you, Wilder."

He ground his teeth together and leaned against the wall.

"You've got all the subtlety of a sledgehammer." I glanced across the gym where a group of older boys were tossing a medicine ball back and forth. "Let me talk to him. He just needs someone to knock some sense into him with a gentler hand."

"A hammer instead of a sledgehammer," he stated with a sneer.

Man, I wanted to slap him right now. *Bad.*

"Listen," I said, leaning closer, "I'm a twenty-five-year-old in the middle of a high school do-over, but for all intents and purposes, I'm one of them… and I've been out there. They trust me with things they don't trust with the faculty. I got into a lot of trouble to earn that, you know."

"Shite." He ran his hand over his face. "I've become an authority figure."

I snorted and rolled my eyes. "*The irony.*"

"Someone attacked that girl," he said. "It wasn't a demon, so it had to be someone from the Academy."

He was just voicing his thoughts now because neither of us had any clue.

"If Trent comes to you, you need to help him, Wilder. He's terrified of asking for anything in case he gets kicked out."

"If he's failing—"

"He's going to make a brilliant Natural," I snapped. "He just needs to learn how to focus. If I remember correctly, that's something you taught me."

"You volunteered me, didn't you?"

"You bet your bulging biceps I did." I punched him in the arm and made a dash for the exit.

"Scarlett!"

Not this time, buddy, I thought. This time I was getting the last word.

15

―――――

After a few days of rigorous punishment—meaning extra classes with my favourite teacher, *Mr. Wilder*—I finally had time to make it back to the library.

I really liked Aiden. He was nice, intelligent, handsome, had a good job, and if I had parents, I'd totally take him home to meet them. He'd get along with Jackson like a house on fire, too. There was no comparing him with Wilder—the two men were as different as night and day.

If I took out all the threads that were weaving through this school in their confusing, looping patterns, having a friend who was outside all of that was a welcomed distraction. A friend who knew tonnes of interesting things was just an added bonus.

I flicked through the card catalogue, the musty smell of paper and silverfish filling my nose. Honestly, I didn't know where to start looking for cyphers and old-fashioned runes. Science? Ancient History? Speculative Fiction?

I ran my fingers over the cards, wondering how people ever dealt with hard copies before computers. I suppose that was one of those pesky first-world problems.

Sighing, I slammed the drawer closed, the sound echoing through the silent library. I turned and looked at Galahad's suit of armour and wondered what he'd do. He'd probably ride in on his white horse with his sword aloft. I wondered if the stories about gallant knights and maidens were really true, or if it was just a rose-coloured flourish on an otherwise bleak time. I mean, what did a whole race of people do when their little bubble was destroyed by demons and their only hope at driving them back was destroyed? Most likely the same thing we were doing now, but with less technology.

Deciding I was in over my head, I ventured back to Aiden's office. The door was open as I approached, but when I nudged it open, it was Madeleine who I found inside.

"Hey," I said, watching as she set down a book on Aiden's desk.

She turned and stared at me. "I was looking for Mr. Thompson, but he isn't here."

"Damn," I cursed. "I was looking for him, too."

"He promised to give me another book," she blurted, which sounded like something he'd do.

I felt a pang of remorse as I met her gaze. I'd been so wrapped up in my own problems, she'd seemed to have faded into the background. The way she'd isolated herself bothered me, but in my search to find the threat hiding at the Academy, I'd been part of the problem.

"Maybe he's in a fancy teacher meeting," I offered.

Madeleine shrugged, then made to step around me, but I wrapped my hand around her arm before she could disappear.

"I know you think I've sold out, but if you need anything you can always come to me," I murmured.

She pulled away, her brow creasing. "Sure. Whatever."

"I know this place is hard and the others are arseholes to you, but I'm reaching out to you, Madeleine. If you want things to change, you have to reach back, okay?"

She lowered her chin, averting her gaze from mine.

"Okay?" I prodded.

"Sure." Another shrug and she was off like a rocket, blasting out of the library so fast I was sure she'd left skid marks behind.

I pinched the bridge of my nose and took a deep breath. If only I knew how to help her come out of the shell she'd been forced into. That was Adelaide's field of expertise, but that woman was as illusive as that bloody sword everyone was searching for.

Deciding I had time to wait, I stepped into Aiden's office and began to read all the framed certificates on the wall. Where there weren't shelves of books, there were hints of all the academic achievements he'd made over the years. There was his Academy graduation certificate with a rather large honours ribbon attached to it. Beside that was a degree from Oxford University. Then a master's and a Doctorate of Philosophy. I wondered what he'd researched to get *that*.

A pile of papers I hadn't noticed before were perched precariously on the end of the already overflowing desk. I wondered if it was something to do with the cypher.

I glanced at the door. I should probably wait for Aiden to come back before sticking my nose where it wasn't appropriate. Looking at the stack of folders, my thoughts went to the coded page in the Codex. The standing stones, the flame symbol, the Order… What if it was a calling card left for the remaining members? I wasn't exactly a part of the alleged secret society, but my parents were probably the last. That meant…

Curiosity won out over sense, and I flicked open the cover of the top creamy manila folder, but what I found inside wasn't quite what I was expecting.

A photograph of a woman sat on the top, the colours faded and the questionable fashion marking it somewhere around the 1980s or 90s. Turning it over, I saw someone had written on the back in pencil. *Andromeda Abernethy, age eighteen.*

This was Aldrich's sister who'd gone missing thirty years ago. He'd said his family had a thing for the letter A, but I didn't know it extended to their surname. They all had the initials A.A., which could be amusing and awkward depending on how you looked at it.

Flipping the picture back, I studied Andromeda. There was something startlingly familiar about her features. She had the same warm chocolate-coloured eyes, the same cascading hair, and her smile... She was younger, but not by much. *You have to hide, Scarlett.*

I closed my eyes, discarding the memory of as quickly as it arose. Could Andromeda be my mother?

Her familiarity almost confirmed it. That meant Aldrich could be my uncle. If that was true, then I wasn't as alone as I once thought.

Don't jump ahead of yourself, Scarlett. You're acting on too many assumptions.

I set the picture down, wondering why Aiden would have a copy of it in his office. Had he been doing more research? I wouldn't put it past him, especially since I knew history gave him a hard on.

Moving the photograph aside, I scanned the papers underneath. Notes were attached to other photos and files with Aiden's scrawling handwriting covering all of them. Yellow Post-its poked out of a tired-looking notebook, and they also covered the back of the manila folder.

Ravenwood is most likely a pseudonym, I read. *Perhaps a name Scarlett was given or she took as a child. There is no reference to it in the Natural heraldry, which suggests her family's identity could have been a matter of secrecy.*

Aiden was researching my family tree? What for? Was this coming from a good place or... I shook my head, clearing the bad thoughts before they entered my mind.

I'd asked him for help to decode the coin, but this? I wasn't sure if it was creepy or extremely helpful.

Why would he keep this to himself? Why wouldn't he just tell me what he was doing? It wasn't like we weren't friends—I'd trusted him with something important. Something that meant life or death for billions of people. Something that the demons would kill to get their hands on. Something… My heart seemed to stop beating for a full thirty seconds.

I opened the folder and began shuffling the papers, my Light ebbing out of my fingertips. There were all kinds of records here. Reports from the London Sanctum—including the one I'd written after the Necropolis—training schedules, progress reports, my file from social services, school records from the various places I'd been throughout my teenage years… He even had a copy of the police report from that one time I'd been arrested as a teenager and released without charge.

I cast them all aside and gasped when I saw a separate folder at the bottom of the pile. There was a telltale emblem on the front and my blood ran cold. *My medical records.*

My skin began to prickle, and I felt like I was going to throw up into the bin beside the desk. What was he doing with all of this? What did it had to do with Arondight or the coin?

I tapped into my Light and let it flow freely around the room. The release of power was like opening a pressure valve and as it trickled around the office, my unease began to grow.

Aiden had gone too far, but why? *Why?*

Think, Scarlett… Why did Greer and Aldrich send you here?

That's when I felt it.

It wasn't just the piles of personal papers that had me reeling. It was the fingerprints all over it. Shadowy, slimy, nauseating. Darkness had been here… and recently.

I glanced at the door, a sudden wave of panic slamming into me, but I was alone and the library was silent. Clearing up the mess I'd made of Aiden's research, I set it back how I found it, or at least as close as I was able.

My whole life I'd never been important, but now I was the centre of everything and I wasn't sure who I could trust. Too many people had more than one face. I let down my guard… I mean, I should be able to amongst my own people, but Wainthrope had taught me an important lesson. *Power corrupts, but absolute power corrupts absolutely.*

I left the office, closing the door behind me. Crossing the library, I lingered between some shelves at the back and screwed my eyes shut. I counted to ten, sucking in breath after breath, settling the burning in my throat.

All this time we'd been looking for a student, and it hadn't occurred to anyone that a teacher could have been compromised.

My only saving grace was that I didn't tell him

about my real reason for being here. To him, I was just a clueless woman trying to get a handle on her powers and place in the world, not a double agent attempting to root out a mutated Natural.

I had to go on like nothing was amiss, though. I had to pretend. If Aiden was mutated, then… He'd chosen it, which made him a Vessel—a willing participant in demonic possession.

Oh, Aiden.

Pulling myself together, I walked out of the library and into the hall beyond.

Outside, the sun was already setting, orange fingers of light streamed through the windows and across the polished terrazzo floors. The days were getting longer as summer approached, but my mood wasn't lifting with the temperature. The sun could be illusive in Britain, kind of like my faith in others.

It was past dinnertime, and Wilder was still in the gym, pumping some serious iron. He sat on the end of a bench, lifting what looked like a five-kilo weight in his right hand. As I approached, everything I felt for him was overshadowed by what I'd have to do after this moment.

"Hey, Purples," Wilder said, not looking up from the movement of the dumbbell in his hand. "Back for more punishment?"

"Wilder…"

His gaze snapped to mine in an instant. When he saw the look on my face, he dropped the weight and rose to his feet.

"What's happened?" he murmured, moving close.

I told him everything. About the research, about the files Aiden had, and about the Darkness I felt all over it. I left nothing out.

When I was done, Wilder took my hand and squeezed.

"You were wrong," I whispered.

"About?"

"How can I survive this war? I'm alone, Wilder. There's nowhere left to turn. I—"

He wrapped his arms around me and held me close, his embrace the only thing that was keeping me from falling apart.

"You're not alone," he whispered. "You never were."

Wilder and Islington followed me down a darkening hall, both men silent for the first time in both their alpha male lives.

The moment I'd walked into the headmaster's office and told him what I'd told Wilder, his annoyance at my presence had dropped, along with his apparent rivalry with his past incarnation. Seemed like I'd done something right for a change.

After finding Aiden's rooms in the southern wing empty and no sign of him in the kitchens, our next stop was the library.

I still didn't understand how I missed this. The only way he could have gone under the radar was if he was working with the demons. The mutation inside him would have been detected if it was always active, so he had to have been fading in and out to maintain his cover.

Islington and I waited outside when Wilder insisted on scouting ahead.

"Thank you," the headmaster said.

I raised an eyebrow.

"I know I've been hard on you, but you were right about a lot of things. Things have gotten too…" he trailed off as the library door opened.

"He's in his office," Wilder murmured.

I nodded and took a step forwards, but he caught my arm.

"Do you want me to come with you?"

"No. I have to do this myself."

He nodded, his eyes flashing silver in the muted light. "We'll be outside, okay?"

"Sure."

I schooled my expression into calmness and strode into the library. Wilder and Islington followed close behind, breaking off and disappearing as soon as they'd crossed the threshold. They lingered amongst the rows of books as I approached Aiden's office, silent watchers in the shadows.

Warm light spilled through of the crack in the office door and I knew Aiden was in there. I could feel his presence just beyond.

Nudging the door open with the toe of my boot, my heart lurched painfully as I saw him bent over his desk, reading intently. Was it more of his creepy research? It hardly mattered now that the net was cast around him.

"Hey," I said.

He looked up, a smile spreading across his face. "Oh, Scarlett, there you are. Madeleine said you were looking for me."

"I was. And now I've found you." I narrowed my eyes, my gaze sliding over the pile of research sitting in full view on his desk.

"What's wrong?" he asked. "Did you find the cypher?"

"No," I replied, moving around him, "but I found something else. It's quite interesting, you know."

I flicked open the cover of the folder directly on top of the pile, uncovering the photograph of Andromeda. Aiden's gaze followed my movements, his face slowly changing colour.

"There are some situations where thorough research would get you points," I began, turning to the next page. "Like PhDs and thesis'. But there are times when it's just downright creepy."

He swallowed hard, a thin sheen of sweat erupting across his forehead. "Scarlett, it's not what you think—"

"I would've given you the benefit of the doubt," I went on, snapping the file closed. "But why does a historian need my medical records? Why does he need my social services file? What does any of that have to do with anything?"

"Arondight," he replied. "You want to find it and I'm trying to help. *I'm trying to help.*"

"Then tell me something," I snarled, slamming the Darkness-soaked folder against his chest. "What do you get out of it? Money? Immunity? A place in the new world order?"

His eyes widened. "What are you talking about?"

"Darkness, Aiden. I'm talking about *Darkness*. *Open your eyes.*"

His breath caught as his fingers brushed against the folder. "*No…*"

"Your fingerprints are all over it." I let out a strangled cry of frustration. "*I trusted you.*"

"This wasn't me, Scarlett!" he cried. "You have to believe me. I gathered the research, but someone else did this. I—"

"I think that's about enough of that," Wilder declared, slipping into the tiny office.

Aiden turned, letting out a yelp as he realised he was trapped between us. "This isn't what you think," he said, becoming increasingly agitated. "You're in danger, Scarlett. Something's in the Academy."

"Oh, we know," Wilder drawled, wrenching Aiden's arms behind his back. The folder fell to the floor, spilling papers across the hardwood.

"Stop!" he cried. "I'd never betray you, Scarlett! I care about you!"

I turned away as Wilder dragged him from the room, fixing my gaze on the antique arondight blade on the shelf.

"I'm sorry, Scarlett," Islington's voice echoed from behind. He'd used my name for the first time, and I bristled, wondering if this meant I'd finally graduated to adult status in his eyes.

"The students have a way through the wards," I said. "I'd hope they'd have enough sense to come to you, but it looks like they didn't. I can't blame them, considering you're so *approachable*. That's likely how the demons have been getting in and out, and why no one's found any trace. The demon tripped the alarm either by accident or was testing the response. Either way, you have to plug the hole because something big is about to go down."

"We will."

"They have everything," I murmured. "Everything we know… It's only a matter of time before someone finds Arondight." And I didn't know who that would be.

"I'm going to summon Greer and the Regula," Islington replied. "Nothing will get into this school and nothing will get to you. Do you understand?"

I drew in a deep breath and nodded. "I think it's time to give me back my arondight blade, don't you?"

16

The entire Academy was summoned to the ballroom the next morning.

As a result, the entire student body was squashed into a space that was meant to handle half the number. Some kids were sitting in groups, others were standing or leaning against the walls. The few window boxes were crammed with bodies, and the air was growing a little too warm for comfort. It seemed as if air vents hadn't been invented in the seventeen-hundreds, along with the ability to open a fancy window in a fancy hall.

My arse was starting to numb from the hardwood underneath my cheeks and I longed for a chair. It seemed like the Academy didn't do school assemblies very often—if at all. There was definitely no drama class that required a stage, or a school band. I snorted, wondering what that'd look like. Probably a million times better than the shite we were forced to perform when I was in high school.

I sat cross-legged beside Trisha, who was talking intently with the other seniors. My arondight blade was pressed comfortingly against my side, hidden underneath my jacket. I hoped I wouldn't have to use it, but if it came to the crunch, I'd whip it out in a flash.

"Something big is happening," Trisha said. "They never call all of us together like this."

"Do you think we're in danger?" Maisy wondered aloud.

"It's gotta be something about that Infernal," Trent replied.

"Andy said they found where that kid was smuggling in the beer and stuff," someone whispered loudly. "Do you think that's where it got in?"

I glanced at Trent and he paled. I would've said I was disappointed in him, but I wasn't even surprised. That kid had a lot to learn about accountability if he was ever going to graduate at the end of the year.

"Did you go to see Wilder?" I hissed, keeping my voice low enough so the others didn't hear.

He gave me a sheepish look.

"*Trent.*"

He opened his mouth but was interrupted by a commotion at the head of the ballroom.

"Listen up!" Islington's voice boomed. "Naturals, stand to attention!"

Everyone stood, forming perfect lines across the breadth of the room and folded their hands behind their backs. I joined them, blending into the swarm of students as the faculty formed a guard at the opposite end.

Adelaide stood next to the headmaster, followed by Masters on his other side, then Patrick and the other combat instructors—including Mr. Wilder—and the various other authority figures. The older woman who taught ethics, the demonology professor, and the teachers of all the other disciplines—history, sciences, and languages. One person in particular was glaringly absent.

"Effective immediately," Islington announced, "the Academy is on high alert."

The room erupted into a burst of hushed whispers.

"Silence!" he shouted, reigning in the one hundred or so students with practiced ease. "Now, more than ever, we must remain vigilant and look out for one another. We must uphold all the virtues bestowed upon us from the Codex and remember why each one of us is here at the Academy."

"For the Light," the students declared in unison.

"For the Light," he echoed. "From this point forwards, all students are confined to the immediate Academy grounds. Wards will be put into place for your safety, and if anyone attempts to test these limits, you will be punished. Am I clear?"

"*Yes, sir!*"

"All students will adhere to their schedules and be signed in and out of all activities, including free study periods. A curfew will be strictly enforced, and you all must sign into your dormitories with your

Light." A few annoyed moans echoed from amongst the students. "Remember, this is for your protection."

A hand rose into the air a few rows ahead of me. "Sir? Are we in danger?"

The headmaster lowered his gaze and took a deep breath before his eyes met the crowd. "Demon activity has been on the rise," he said. "Every student here is our future, and our future must be protected." The murmuring began again, but this time Islington didn't put a stop to it. "Return to your classes, but remain vigilant. Dismissed."

The students fell out of three ranks and the volume began to increase as they talked furiously amongst one another. As we all moved towards the door, the heaviness in the air increased.

"You were right, Scarlett," Trisha said. "Something's coming, isn't it?"

"I hope not," I murmured. *For all our sakes.*

"They never tell us anything," Kayla said with a pout. "They just bark orders at us and expect us to jump."

"That's what being a Natural is all about," I said. "We're soldiers and we must work together. That's the only hope we have against the Darkness."

She narrowed her eyes at me, obviously thinking her way was better and led the seniors out of the ballroom. I hung back, attempting to quell my annoyance at her continued temper tantrums. You think she'd have learned something by now.

Catching sight of Wilder at the head of the room,

I wove through a few stragglers so I could catch him before he left.

"Hey."

Wilder stopped when he heard my voice and turned. I stood in front of him, glancing as the last of the students filed past us.

"Islington has summoned the London council," he told me once they'd gone. "They'll be here by nightfall."

"And the Regula?"

"They're sending a representative. They'll interrogate Aiden, then likely hand him over to Ramona and her team."

"Can the mutation be reversed?" I wasn't sure I wanted to know the answer, knowing that he'd willingly worked with the shadow that was growing inside his body.

I hadn't seen a Vessel since the first night I'd met Wilder and I still didn't understand it. Was it a power thing? There was no logical explanation for someone being a willing host to a demon, let alone a parasitic mutation.

"We won't know until Ramona can do an assessment." He shrugged, his expression giving away that he thought it was hopeless.

What would become of Aiden? But I already knew the answer—he'd be executed.

"Keep an eye on that lot," Wilder said, nodding towards the hallway where the students had exited.

"I will," I said, following his gaze. "I won't let anything happen to them."

A full day of classes hadn't softened anyone's nerves, least of all mine.

As far as I could tell, Greer or the Regula representative hadn't arrived yet, which only added to my worry. London wasn't that far away. What if something had happened to them en route?

I stepped into the ruined chapel, the quiet of the early evening was unsettling, but the moment I passed over the threshold, I felt an odd sense of calm. Light must be interwoven in the stone here.

I moved up the centre of the room and chose a spot on a pew at the front, perching directly opposite the altar. The stone was cold on my arse, but the connection to this place was stronger that way. The Lady of the Lake watched over me with her marble eyes, her silence deafening.

Ivy wrapped around her body, the vines snaking upwards around her outstretched arms. She was a formidable figure frozen in the midst of a battle cry. I wondered what had happened to her. Something must've, because where was she now? Not here where the Naturals needed her the most.

"Scarlett?"

I turned, my heart leaping into my throat. I sighed in relief as I caught sight of Madeleine lingering at the back of the chapel.

"Hey," I said, my voice echoing off the stone. "You scared the absolute crap outta me."

"Sorry," she said, shuffling forwards.

I looked her over, sensing something was amiss. "Is everything okay?"

"Can…" She took a deep breath. "Can I sit with you?"

"Of course." I patted the stone next to me and she sat, shoving her hands underneath her thighs. "What's up?"

"You said I could talk to you," she began, her shoulders hunched. "I was hoping…"

"I'm all ears," I declared with a smile.

Madeleine fell into silence, her entire body tense. I waited, allowing her to gather her thoughts in her own time. Forcing her to let out all her issues wouldn't help anyone. Besides, the simple fact that she'd gathered enough courage to come to me was enough.

"You've been through so much," she murmured after a long moment, her eyes misting. "How are you so strong?"

"Sometimes I wonder that myself," I replied. "But I think it comes down to the choices I made. I don't have to sit down and take the bad stuff. I can choose to stand up and fight."

"What if it's unavoidable? What if the choice is taken away from you?"

I hesitated, shivering as the air turned cold. My gaze met hers. "Madeleine?"

She choked back a sob and grasped my hand, a sharp bolt of electricity passing between us. Her Light sparked abrasively against mine, a hint of Darkness reacting to the shard of Arondight lodged within me.

How did I miss this? I'd seen so much of her in

myself, I'd ignored what was right in front of me, that's how. I believed what I'd wanted to.

"How?" I whispered, my heart breaking. *Two Naturals, not one...* "Do you remember being possessed?"

She shook her head, tears welling in her eyes. "I'm so scared, Scarlett."

"I know, but you have to tell me everything you can. Whatever's going on here, we have to stop it."

"I don't remember," she said. "I started losing time. A few hours here and there. I'd wake up tired and things would go missing in my room. Then I started losing entire days, and one day... I started to see things."

"See things?"

"Like someone else was living my life and I was trapped inside, watching, helpless. I knew something had a hold of me, but there was nothing I could do. I fought it, Scarlett, I really did... but it fed off my misery."

"That's why you attacked Kayla." *Oh, Madeleine...*

"It wasn't me," she cried. "It's this *thing* inside me."

"Human Convergence," I whispered.

"What?"

How did I tell her she was possessed by an Infernal who infected her with a possible irreversible mutation? *Gently.*

"Madeleine..." I sighed. "There's no easy way to say this. You were possessed by an Infernal who infected you with something that's taking control of your body."

"What?" She stared at me with big eyes and I grasped her shoulders.

"The same thing happened to my best friend Jackson. I don't know what's going to happen next, but I know some people who can help you."

"They can fix me?" she whispered. "It doesn't feel like it'll ever go away."

"I don't know… but you have to keep fighting, okay?" She nodded and I offered her a reassuring smile. "We have to go find Wilder."

She paled. "Mr. Wilder?"

I nodded. "He'll help us get back to the London Sanctum. The doctor there, Ramona… she's great. And you can meet Jackson. He's really good at the whole strength thing." I rose to my feet and gestured for her to come.

"But…" she glanced at the door then back to me, her anxiety etched deep on her face, "I'm…"

"Don't worry, I'll take care of you."

She stood, wavering from side to side, then her hand shot out and she grasped my upper arm. "Scarlett, wait."

Her skin had turned a sickly shade of grey and she lurched forwards as if something was twisting her stomach.

I held her steady, my heart racing. "Madeleine?"

"They know everything," she blurted, trying to force the words out of her mouth. The mutation must be trying to stop her. "The coin, the Order, who Mr.

Thompson thinks your mother is, that you hold a shard of Arondight… They know all of it. They know everything about you.”

“They know about the shard?” I asked with a shake of my head. “I never told anyone about that.”

“The thing inside me can sense it,” she said, her eyes wild. “They want you, Scarlett. Above all else, *they want you.*”

It was then that I realised Madeleine had been in Aiden’s office right before I’d found all of his research. It was the shadow who’d left Darkness there in an attempt to frame him and buy more time. That meant Aiden was innocent. *Aiden was innocent…*

“The coin is the key,” Madeleine hissed, her fingers biting into my skin.

“The key to what?”

“To the resting place of Arondight,” she rasped. “The key, the shard, and the stones.”

I stared at her, the pieces falling into place. The coin must be a key and I was the only one who could use it. As for the standing stones, wherever they were hidden, that’s where we’d find Arondight.

The race was well and truly on, but I had two out of the three pieces they believed we needed.

“We need to get you to safety,” I said. “Can you walk?”

“I can feel it trying… to take… *over…*” She grimaced, and I tightened my grip.

“I’m not going to leave you, okay?” I soothed. “We’re going to find Wilder and we’re getting you out of here.”

Tears began to fall from her eyes. "I'm scared."

I didn't have any words to reassure her. Instead, I helped her move towards the exit. The only thing we could do was get her to Ramona as fast as we were able.

"*Scarlett… I can't…*" Madeleine let out a wail and her fingers clawed at her head. "*Help me…*"

The teen began to convulse as she fought the monster inside her, her consciousness seeming to fade from one to the other.

"Madeleine!" I slapped her across the face, my palm stinging. "Fight it!"

Her head snapped to the side, and when she turned back towards me, her eyes began to swirl and shift into two black orbs. Her lips curved into an evil grin, and I knew the mutation inside her had taken control. Was this the fate that'd been waiting for Jackson? *Oh, Madeleine…*

"It's too late," the shadow rasped. "The girl is gone, and it's only a matter of hours until everyone here is ripped apart."

"What are you talking about?" I demanded, shaking it. Madeleine's head lolled back and forth, the creature inside her laughing. "*Tell me!*"

"The key, the shard, the stones…" it chortled. "It's a fine night for a *cataclysm*."

"*No…*"

They wanted to destabilise the Naturals by going for their children… and I'd done all the research on Arondight they need to move forward. Now I was alone with the shadow, in prime position to be snatched by the demons. Three birds, one stone.

A piercing shriek tore through the air, followed by a long wail that throbbed deep in my eardrums. I slapped my hands over my ears, stumbling backwards.

The alarms!

"It's already begun," the shadow declared, moving towards me. "You belong to us now, Scarlett Ravenwood. Death is upon you."

A burst of Darkness slammed into me and I was hurled into the air, twisting over and over until I hit the wall of the chapel with a bang. I landed hard, the air pushing out of my lungs.

"I'm not letting you take me," I rasped, dragging myself across the floor, "and I'm definitely not letting you take Madeleine."

The shadow loomed over me. "It's over, Natural. You belong to us now."

"*Nuh ah*," I declared, pushing to my knees. "You said it yourself. *I've got the shard.*"

I launched upwards, ramming my shoulder into the shadow's gut and we hurtled across the chapel, propelled by a burst of indigo Light. The creature shrieked with Madeleine's voice, attempting to call on its Darkness, but I was faster.

As we collided with the altar, I grabbed its shoulders as we rolled. Thankfully, I landed on top, and with one swift movement, I'd flipped my cold iron dagger into my hand and struck.

I rammed it through the shadow's shoulder, the

blade sinking through flesh and bone, finally embedding into the stone beneath.

The creature wailed and thrashed in pain, but it was well and truly stuck. The Naturals were fighting back, and the power that was bound within the stone beneath us held the demon in its grasp. It wasn't going anywhere anytime soon, that's for sure.

Madeleine's eyes flashed, returning to their Natural state, and she screamed, her hands clawing at the dagger.

"*Scarlett*," she cried, her body shuddering in pain.

"I'm sorry, Madeleine," I murmured, smoothing back her hair. "The alarms have sounded, which means—"

"We're under attack."

I nodded.

"I'm sorry," she whispered. "*I'm so sorry.*"

"I know. It isn't your fault, you hear? *This isn't your fault.*"

Her mouth opened and closed, and I could tell from the look in her eyes that she blamed herself. Maybe she would for a long time if she came out the other side of this.

"You'll be safe here," I said, reaching for my arondight blade. "When this is over, I'll come back for you, okay? Then we'll go to London together."

She nodded, her bottom lip trembling. "Scarlett?"

"Yeah?"

"I don't want to die."

My heart twisted and I moved to my knees. Stroking her hair away from her face, I took her hand

and squeezed. "You're not going to die, Madeleine. I'm going to go kick some demon arse, then we'll go see the doc, okay?"

Her eyes drooped and she swallowed hard.

"Just hang tight, okay?"

"*Okay…*"

As I ran from the chapel and out into the night, I wondered if I'd just made her a promise I couldn't keep.

17

———

Sprinting across the lawn, I made my way towards the Academy.

The alarms were still wailing, the sound tearing my eardrums to pieces. A shriek pierced through the unbearable sound, and I whirled, my boots skidding on the grass.

The horizon was streaked with the ominous colours of a fiery sunset—all red and orange, mixed with the fading blue of the spring sky.

A bright pulse of Light drew my attention to the north, where I also found a writhing mass of lesser demons streaking across the grounds.

Shite. The wards were down, which meant nothing was protecting the Academy's borders.

I changed course, doing what I did best—run headfirst into danger.

I brought my arondight blade to life, trailing violet sparks in my wake. Sprinting through the first wave of lesser demons, I swung, striking with deadly precision.

I cried out as my sword cut through bone and sinew, the rotting corpses collapsing in on themselves as their demon hosts bit the proverbial dust.

The sickly stench of rot filled the air as several of the possessed corpses turned and charged. I leapt, pirouetting and cutting down anything that came within reach. I knew if they were able to get onto the grounds, nothing would stop them from overrunning everything in their path.

They must not reach the Academy buildings, or they'd destroy everything we'd worked for. The students, the teachers, and the relics inside the library were all under threat.

Another scream tore through the air, and I cried out as I cut down the last lesser demon. Its flesh bubbled and spit as my arondight blade severed its head from its retch-inducing shoulders. The shell the demon inhabited used to be a human once, which didn't make fighting them any easier, but at least their soul had already departed their body. The humans the lessers took over were spared that fate at least.

Jumping over the carnage, I ran towards the scream, my breath heaving and burning my lungs— and I thought I was getting used to all the physical exertion in this place.

That's when I saw Trent and Kayla surrounded and unarmed, fighting back a group of lesser demons with their Light.

I charged, taking the enemy by surprise, and cut them down one by one.

Hands grabbed Kayla from behind, and she

screamed as her head was wrenched back. Teeth darted for her jugular and I sprung, slamming my blade through the demon's skull. I pulled back as the corpse crumpled to the lawn, and Kayla fell against the wall with a cry.

"Are you okay?" I asked, grasping her shoulder with my free hand.

She nodded, her eyes glassy. "I-I think so."

I glanced around, checking for movement, but all was still. My training told me that we'd just experienced the first wave of many. The scouts—or the cannon fodder as Wilder called them—were testing our defences, looking for weak points to exploit before sending in the heavy artillery.

Long story short, the shite had not even hit the fan yet.

"I think that's all of them for now," I said. "Let's get you two inside."

Trent slung his arm around Kayla's waist, and we began to move around the side of the building towards the gym.

A shockwave rumbled through the ground and I held up my hand, halting the others.

"What's that?" Kayla asked.

Trent glanced at me. "It feels like an earthquake."

The ground shook again, and this time, it kept going. *Boom, boom, boom, boom...* like approaching footsteps of doom.

"It's a Colossus!" Trent exclaimed, jabbing his finger across the grounds.

I followed his wild gestures and my heart stopped

as I saw what was making all the mini-earthquakes. A giant mass was lumbering towards us, its clubbed fists swinging back and forth.

It had to be over twelve feet tall, its body made up of stitched together clumps of flesh and steel plates. Even from this distance, I could feel the electric charge pulsing through the mass of muscle and sinew. Inside, I knew there was a ball of Darkness powering the lumbering mass and it was being controlled by something more potent.

Its head was fat and distorted with tufts of hair sticking up in all directions. Bulbous eyeballs protruded out of its hashed-up skull, and its mouth was on an unnatural slant. I didn't want to even get started with its teeth.

So this was the Colossus Aldrich fought solo at the Sanctum? *Holy cow…*

"Run!" I commanded. "Get to the gym. I'll hold it off."

Trent's eyes were almost falling out of his head with fear. "But—"

"I said run!" I felt the shard of Arondight flare inside me, and for a split-second, the world was tinted violet.

Their eyes widened and they turned, making their way towards the gym. I followed them a short distance, intending to draw the Colossus across the lawn and away from the Academy, but as we rounded the corner, a wall of demons were waiting for us.

Their glassy eyes stared at us, their bent and broken limbs dangling at odd angles. The sound of laboured breathing filled the air and I grasped Trent's arm, pulling the students behind me.

"What now?" he hissed, his voice breaking.

"Follow my lead," I replied. "If anything comes at you, push it back with your Light."

"I really wish we had arondight blades," Kayla whispered with tears in her eyes. Yeah, so did I.

We moved backwards, inching away from the line of demons. Their beady eyes were glued to us, but they didn't attack, they just edged creepily after us like a wall of lumbering, disinterested zombies. Something was controlling them.

We'd have to cut through the building, risking a breach of the administration wing, but there was no other way around without drawing the ire of the giant lumbering across the lawn.

The ground shook as the Colossus approached, my heartbeat accelerating with every tremor. Aldrich was a master warrior with decades of experience under his belt. I was just a girl with barely a year of training, an unknown power inside of me, and a reckless streak that'd probably get me killed one day. How could I take on a Colossus on my own? I couldn't.

Everything was about to go wrong if I didn't get us out of here.

I rushed up to the door leading into the hallway that joined the admin building to the classrooms and yelped as rotting hands and faces slammed against the glass.

"They're inside!" Kayla cried.

Trent spat out an extremely dirty word that would curl even the Darkest of demon's hair.

With nowhere else to go, we were edged out into the open towards the Colossus. I had to fight it, there was no other way.

We were in so much trouble.

The demons began to circle around our position, trapping us inside the eye of the storm with the lumbering beast. Their jaws snapped as their feet churned up the lawn, their clicking and wailing filled the air with Darkness.

"Trent," I grasped his arm, my fingers biting into his skin, "you cast a shield over you and Kayla before. Can you do it again?"

"Yeah, but—"

"I need you to do it now. Join together and protect yourselves." I looked at Kayla, who nodded.

"What about you?" she asked.

"I'll be fine." *Maybe.* "I've got an arondight blade and a little of the real thing. The others are coming. I just need to hold it off until they do, okay?"

The wailing reached a fever pitch as the Colossus fixed its gaze on us.

"It's time to prove to me you're in this for the long haul," I told Trent. "This is your moment."

He swallowed hard and nodded. "Got it. I won't let you down."

I flicked my wrist, making sure my arondight blade was well and truly engaged. "*Now.*"

Light erupted from within Trent as he knelt, tugging Kayla down beside him. She joined her power with his and a spark of silver bloomed overhead before shimmering into a silver dome that closed them off from the horde.

I whirled as the demons shrieked, then the Colossus let out a roar of anger that shook me to my very core.

Tensing, I charged the seven-foot-tall wall of steel and flesh, my gaze searching for any weak spots in its armour. It swung its clubbed fist at me, and I threw myself backwards, skidding feet-first underneath its meaty arm. I raised my sword and clipped it below the elbow, drawing a spray of congealed black blood.

The Colossus wailed and twisted, searching for me, but I was already on my feet, striking the back of its knees. Violet sparks erupted, filling the air with the stench of metal and blood as I struck the steel plates infused within its pieced-together body.

Crying out in frustration, I cursed the fact that there hadn't been a class on how to defeat this pile of rotting shite. If I got out of this, I'd be filling up the suggestion box outside Islington's office with all the feedback cards I could get my hands on.

The Colossus flailed wildly, its fist striking me in the side. I was flung into the air, then hit the ground hard, the wind pushing out of my lungs as I rolled towards the wall of lesser demons still circling us. I rolled, then was kicked back into the centre. Pain tore through my ribs as I gasped for breath, Trent and Kayla's cries fading into the background as blood whooshed in my ears.

An ugly, distorted face appeared over me, casting

the darkening sky into shadow. The Colossus loomed, its stubby fingers reaching out towards me.

I gasped, searching for Arondight. It didn't reply and I roared, rolling to the side as a massive fist slammed into the ground where my head had been a moment before.

What was happening? Had I used everything the shard had given me already? Why wasn't it answering?

I pushed to my feet, giving the Colossus a wide berth. I had my Light, right? I couldn't rely on a power I knew nothing about to get us through this, and there was no way of knowing if Wilder and the others were coming. This was on me. Trent and Kayla's lives depended on what I did next.

Talk about a tall order.

The Colossus whirled, its size making the movement seem as if it was in perpetual slow motion.

"Has anyone ever told you how ugly you are?" I shouted at it. "Someone gave you a pretty big whack with the ugly stick."

The creature roared, seemingly understanding the insult. *Wow, I didn't see that one coming.*

I wiped the back of my hand across my nose, grimacing as it came back streaked with blood. *Didn't see that one coming, either.*

"Hey, you sack of rotting maggot flesh!" I shouted. "Yo mama's so stupid, she yelled into an envelope to send a voicemail!"

The Colossus swung and I ducked. The blow sailed over my head, the force buffeting my hair. I twisted, my sword cutting into a piece of soft flesh under its arm.

"Yo mama's so fat that when she fell over, she rocked herself asleep trying to get up again."

"*Brutal...*" I heard Trent say somewhere behind me.

I dodged another blow, darting in and slicing wherever I could reach.

"Yo mama's so fat, she doesn't need the internet because she's already worldwide!"

The beast bashed its fists on the ground, sending up a spray of dirt. A clump of grass narrowly missed my head and I tensed. I had to drop this thing like yesterday.

Summoning all of my strength, I launched myself at the Colossus, leaping into the air. I landed on its back, my fist curling around a slice of metal protruding out of its shoulder blade. I hung on for dear life as the monster began to thrash and flail, my grip slipping.

I let out a roar and stabbed my arondight blade into a slice of unprotected flesh over the Colossus' spine. Light-infused steel cut through rotting flesh like butter, imbedding right to the hilt. I dug my heels into its back and twisted my sword, praying for a miracle.

The effect was immediate. The Colossus jerked, its cry of pain reverberated through my bones, then it was falling.

Its spine was severed and everything below the neck was useless.

I stood over it, watching as it twitched. Darkness-infused eyes met mine and a black tongue rolled out of its Frankenstein mouth. I knew it was a monster—an entity pieced together by Darkness so foul it left a bad taste in my mouth—but I couldn't leave it like this.

Holding my breath, I wrenched my sword free, then lifted it over my head. With a strangled cry, I brought it down on the Colossus' neck. Once, twice, three times, then it was dead.

The circle of lesser demons stopped in their tracks, their beady, vacant eyes staring at me.

"Who's next?" I asked as I turned. "As you can see, I don't need a single drop of Arondight to fight you." I held out my sword, brandishing the point at every demon who dared face me.

There had to be at least fifty of the things around us, and those were the ones I could see.

"You're not going to kill me or them," I said. "I'm too important to your master. You need the shard."

I took a step towards the wall of flesh.

"Scarlett," Trent called, "what are you doing?"

"You will let us pass," I commanded the demons. "If you don't, only death awaits you."

The demons snapped and moaned, then edged aside, creating an opening.

I gestured for Trent and Kayla. "C'mon, let's split before they change their minds."

Trent let their shield dissipate and helped Kayla to her feet. We slunk through the gap, my heart beating uneasily as the demons watched our passing. My side burned, likely from a few broken ribs, but I ignored the pain—along with the throb in my right leg—and kept moving.

"*Creepy*," Kayla whispered.

"More like stinky," Trent answered.

When we were clear, I ordered them to keep walking and not to look back. Too bad I didn't follow my own advice, because what I saw was going to haunt me for the rest of my life.

I glanced over my shoulder at the mass of lesser demons and shivered. They were just standing there, staring after us, nothing more than vacant, expressionless zombies. Their clothes were torn and stained with old blood, their skin was splotched with grey and black rot, and there were some that only had half a face—the other side had fallen off.

I was in Puke City, population me.

"Scarlett!" Trent called, his voice breaking through the nausea. "There's more coming up the hill!"

"*Shite.*"

Knowing I had an edge, it was my duty to be the sword that protected the Academy from whatever—or whoever—was controlling the horde. A greater demon was out there, pulling the strings, searching for the key and the shard. If I offered them what they wanted, maybe they'd spare the students.

I was playing right into their hands, but I needed to buy some more time until Wilder and the other teachers could find me.

"Get inside," I said, waving towards the Academy. "I'll hold them off."

"We can't leave you again," Kayla exclaimed.

Turning, I grasped her arm, sending a pulse of Arondight's Light into her. The shock bolstered her energy and her eyes widened. Now she understood.

"We'll send help," she said, tugging on Trent's hand.

I nodded and spun around, readying my arondight blade as the horde advanced up the rise. One crazy, purple-haired woman against an army of demons. What could go wrong? *Everything.*

I led them away from the gym towards the front of the grounds. I could see the fountain ahead, the statue of the Lady of the Lake appearing through the gloom. My leg was screaming at me, my limp slowing me down. At least the demons were just following, not attacking.

I was within sight of the front entrance of the Academy when several shadows broke away from the fountain and slunk towards me. They circled and I spun this way and that, but there was no escape—I was trapped.

My heart twisted and I knew what these creatures had been. Humans—men and women infected with the mutation developed by Human Convergence. This was the fate that had been awaiting Jackson and Madeleine.

I choked back a sob. It was too late for them, and now it was too late for me. Now all I could do one of two things—let them take me or fight to the death.

No prizes for guessing which one I chose.

I held my arondight blade aloft and launched

myself at the closest shadow, but it dodged my blow with ease. It dipped, then counter struck, its shadowy fist slamming into my jaw. I fell to my knees, stars erupting through my vision.

They closed in on me, another inky figure kicking me in the side. I landed on my back, dazed as I stared up at the blank faces which loomed over me. There was nothing there—no eyes, no mouth, no nose… just Darkness. There was nothing left of who they used to be.

I drew in a shaky breath as their slimy hands reached for me.

"*Wilder*…" I whispered. "*Wilder… I… I'm* sorry…"

White Light sliced through the shadows, cutting down the wave of Darkness with deadly accuracy. Wails filled the air as the creatures exploded into a shower of flame and ash, and I clamped my hands over my ears as the sound tore at my eardrums.

"Scarlett."

Opening my eyes, I sucked in breath after breath.

I almost expected to see Wilder standing over me, but it wasn't him at all. It was the last person I expected to see.

"Brax?"

18

———

B rax turned, looking rather unimpressed, and flicked his arondight blade. Blood and guts splattered onto the ground as the sword clicked back into the hilt. He held out his hand with a sigh. Somehow, I felt like there was another detention coming.

I grasped his wrist and he hauled me to my feet. "Thanks."

"It seems like I arrived just in time," he said, his tone clipped. "Do you want to explain what's going on here?"

I narrowed my eyes. If he'd seen me take down that Colossus, he wouldn't be saying that. Actually, whatever he said would be in the exact same tone. It was a lose-lose situation with this guy. He was the perfect candidate to be a politician if you asked me.

"Demons," I replied. "That's what's going on."

"*Obviously.*"

I cast my gaze over the piles of lesser demons and

the scorch marks left behind by their cousins. "Where would you like me to start?" I went on. "The bit with the Human Convergence, or the part where I got detention?"

"Where are the others?" he asked, ignoring me. "Islington and the faculty?"

"They've fallen back to the gym," I replied glancing over my shoulder. "The students are there."

"Good," he muttered, "they're all in one place."

I turned, confused by his words, and before I could ask what our game plan should be, his hand shot out and his fingers curled around my neck.

I gasped as he squeezed, a peculiar mix of Light flowing into my body. My fingers and toes began to go numb, and I panicked. Thrashing against his hold, I sensed Darkness within him and pushed back with my indigo Light.

Wilder's doubts flashed through my mind and I slammed my wrist against Brax's elbow. *He wasn't at the Sanctum when we faced Wainthrope.*

His arm buckled, loosening his fingers, and I twisted out of his grasp. Sucking in breath after breath, I reached for my arondight blade, but Brax moved with impossible speed, knocking the hilt out of my hand. It skidded across the gravel, coming to rest at the foot of the fountain.

"You've betrayed us," I rasped, "just like Wainthrope. If you were there, the thread from Markzoth would have linked you to him and you would have been *done*."

Brax wrenched me close, his hand biting into my

upper arm. Darkness pulsated around him and I could taste the metallic tang of it on my tongue—like copper and molten steel.

"Wainthrope was a fool," he snarled. "A weak puppet ripe to be exploited by the one flaw all Naturals have."

"What flaw?" I snorted and gritted my teeth.

"*Love.*"

"Wainthrope and love don't belong in the same sentence."

His lips curved upwards. "It depends on what you love." And for the late Inquisitor, that'd been power.

I blew through my lips. "And what's your excuse, Brax?"

"Think about it, Scarlett." He started to drag me across the courtyard, my boots scraping along the gravel. "Think *really hard.*"

I pulled against him, but his grip was like cold iron, acidic and absolute. What did he mean? Was he a Vessel harbouring something else, or had he taken on power gifted to him from a greater demon? Or had Human Convergence sunk its claws into his flesh?

Even as I cast one theory away for another, I knew something more lingered inside him. Brax had always been cold and distant, his behaviour attributed to his clinical military stance, but he'd never been on my side, or Greer's for that matter. He'd never touched anyone that I remembered, and he was never around, save for all the important council meetings. When Wainthrope had shown up at the London Sanctum, Brax had been right up the Inquisitor's arsehole.

There was only one logical conclusion and I felt like throwing up. It wasn't betrayal—it was the furthest thing from one there could be.

My eyes widened. "You're not Brax…"

"This world was made for us to devour," he rasped. "How easy it is to slide into your kind and feast on your *pathetic souls*."

"Who are you?" I demanded. "Where's Brax?"

"The one you call Brax has been gone for a long time, *Natural*. I control his flesh now."

I stared into his eyes, my throat tightening and my heart galloping at an alarming pace. Did the demon mean that Brax's soul…

"You took his soul," I whispered. "You—"

"His soul is obliterated," he snarled.

"No!" The gravity of what'd happened to Brax— the real Brax—tore through me, the pain insurmountable. It was as if he'd been erased from history, his soul lost, never to return, never to rest… as if he never was. Was this the fate for the human race?

Had I ever known the real Brax, or was it this creature the whole time?

"Who are you?" I demanded for the second time. "I command you to tell me!"

"You cannot command me, child!" The back of his hand collided with my face and I fell to the ground, stars bursting across my vision.

I spat blood, gravel digging into my palms.

"*I am the One*." He moved towards me. "I am the pinnacle." I scrambled towards the fountain, hoping I was moving in the right direction. "I am death, destruction, and *pain.*" My back hit the edge of the fountain and I reached blindly. "I am here to take your world." My fingers brushed against my arondight blade. "With you, I can open the rift between our worlds and let the horde raze your pathetic existence to the ground. Arondight will be your downfall and our triumph!"

I willed my blade into life with a cry and swung, purple sparks showering across the courtyard. Brax— or whoever he was now—stumbled, my swing missing. He engaged his sword, and as his Light manifested the links, I could see a tinge of red glowing along the steel. *How in the hell could he still use his Light?*

I propelled myself to my feet, raising my sword as his came at me, and they collided with a blow so hard, it vibrated up both my arms and rattled my teeth.

Sparks showered everywhere, blinding me to the world around us. We were locked together, my shard of Arondight the only thing holding against the onslaught.

"Scarlett!"

"Stop!" I screamed as Wilder approached from somewhere on my left.

I could see his form through the rain of sparks, his sword at the ready. He looked at Brax, then at me, clearly confused.

"It's not him," I shouted. "Brax is gone."

"Don't listen to her!" Brax barked. "She's been taken!"

"Shut up!" I shouted at Brax. "What was it you

were saying about eating all of our souls? C'mon, it was only two minutes ago."

"Wilder!" Brax roared. "We must stop her or all is lost!"

"The root of all evil," I said, my gaze locking onto his. We were locked so close together, I could see his nose hairs. "That's what you are. The king of the demons, lord of bad breath, duke of rancid body odour. *How dare you take Brax's soul.*"

I pushed against him, breaking apart our swords. Steel slid against steel, and we both struck at the same time, clashing once more.

Our blades locked, then I was forced to move as a third slammed through Brax's chest, directly through his heart. *Wider!*

Brax screamed, his voice shredding the air as flames erupted inside his body. He exploded, the force sent me reeling. I fell against the fountain and tumbled to the ground, my chest heaving.

"You okay?" Wilder stood over me.

"Nice decision you made there," I drawled.

He held out his hand and hauled me to my feet. "I know you better than you think, Purples. No one else is that creative with their insults."

"How did you find me?" I asked, dusting myself off.

"You're still being tracked."

Well, shite. That damn Light tracker was useful for something after all.

"We have to go back to the chapel," I said. "I left Madeleine there."

"Madeleine?"

"She was mutated, Wilder. She was the shadow, but she was strong enough to fight it and come to me for help. We were there when the alarms went off, and I pinned her down with my dagger. If there's a chance of saving her, we have to try."

He raised an eyebrow but didn't offer any smart-arse quips to punctuate my sentence. "We better get her then, Purples."

"What about the demons?"

"Look." He pointed across the grounds where a herd of lesser demons were galloping across the lawn in a hasty retreat. "Without Brax..." He glanced at the blackened mark on the ground. "Without their leader, they'll scatter four ways to the wind."

I could see the faculty was already emerging from the Academy buildings, their arondight blades at the ready. Masters, Patrick, and Adelaide were amongst them, dishing out orders. A group began to give chase to the retreating demons, and the others were sent to scout for stragglers. Before long, the grounds would be clear and the wards restored.

"It's nice not being on our own, huh?" Wilder asked. "We don't have to worry about clean-up duty."

"Very funny." I stormed across the courtyard, pushing away Brax's fate for the time being, knowing I'd have to explain it to Greer and the others. Right now, Madeleine needed my help.

When we got to the chapel, I burst into the sanctuary, the Light infused in the foundation soothing my raging power. But when I turned to the altar, I realised it was empty. Madeleine was gone.

"She was right here," I said, fisting my hands into my hair. "I pinned her right in front of the altar."

"Well, she got free," Wilder said, stating the obvious.

I grabbed his shoulders and shook him. "Wilder, they want the coin."

"The coin?"

"It's the key to finding Arondight. The key, the shard, and the stones."

"And you're the shard."

"Aiden said he knows where the standing stones might be." *Which meant he was the demon's next target.*

I spotted my cold iron dagger on the floor and snatched it up.

"He's locked up tight, Purples. Nothing's getting to him." His hand brushed my waist, the gesture a little too intimate for my liking.

"Madeleine still has some control over her Light," I argued.

"Purples… you're too precious," he murmured, his fingers tightening on my hip. "This is what the shadow wants. It's luring you into a trap."

"I know it's a bloody trap."

"Let us handle it. You'll be safe here. This place is infused with Light."

"But Madeleine still got out…" It was in that moment, where I'd caught just enough of my breath back, that I realised what he was doing. I bristled and slapped his hand away. He was trying to use my feelings to manipulate me into staying in the chapel because he knew I'd do that whole run-head-first-into-danger thing I was so fond of. *How dare he.*

"I saw you!" I shouted, tearing away from him. "I saw you and Greer, Wilder. You can't use my feelings against me anymore. I'm going to do what I think is right, not what you manipulate me into."

He stared at me like I'd just punched him in the face.

"I get it," I ranted. "You don't have to keep bashing me over the head with it, okay? You love Greer, so what? Right now, this is about the demons getting their hands on Arondight and a girl who's scared out of her bloody mind!"

"Scarlett—"

"She's going for Aiden," I snapped. "She'll either take him or kill him, and I'm not going to let that girl become a murderer against her will." Curling my lip, I looked him over. "You can do whatever the hell you want."

I took off, sprinting from the chapel and across the lawn. Wilder appeared beside me, his expression grim.

"The cellar," he said. "Underneath the back building."

Our boots crunched on gravel as we legged it across the courtyard, opening a side door and barrelling across a hallway, before emerging outside again. I skidded around the corner and almost slammed into a lesser demon. My arondight blade sparked and I sliced through its gut, severing it in two without breaking stride.

Wilder took the lead and slammed his shoulder against the door to the northern-most building. I skidded down the hall, my damp boots slipping on the polished floorboards and clattered down the stairs to the cellar below.

The air changed the moment we descended below ground level. It was cold, dank, and metallic. *Madeleine*.

I turned the corner, the row of cells wreathed in inky, unnatural, shadow.

"At the end," Wilder said, urging me forwards.

I kept moving, forging through the Darkness, my stomach turned and my lungs burned as I breathed in the poisonous air. It stank of Sulphur the closer we got, and as we broke through the haze, so did the sound of Aiden's screams.

The bars to his cell had been twisted and pried open, exposing him to the shadow. Madeleine—or the thing she'd become—fisted her hand into his hair and slammed his skull against the dense bluestone. He fought against her with his Light, but the mutation inside her was too strong.

"Madeleine!" I shrieked. "Fight it!"

I grabbed the back of her T-shirt and hauled her off Aiden. She turned on me, her eyes dark and her skin swirling with mottled red and black splotches. I almost recoiled, but I slammed her against the wall, ignoring the pain that throbbed through my body.

"Madeleine!" I cried. "Fight back, damn it! Fight back!"

She let out an agonised wail even as she clawed at me, her fingernails dragging across my skin.

"Scarlett!" Wilder shouted as he dragged Aiden out of the way. "She's gone. Stand back—"

"*No*," I shrieked. "No, I won't let it take her. *I won't--*"

I called on my Light, praying that the shard of Arondight would answer. It had when I'd healed Jackson and when I'd destroyed Markzoth. This was why Arondight existed—to help those survive against the Dark.

The Light must prevail. *It must…*

I poured my Light into Madeleine, the power burning through me, eating my insides with pure indigo flame. I reached out for the dying spark inside her, begging her to come back before it was too late.

Madeleine… it's not your time…

A flash of silver Light glinted in the Darkness and shot towards me, its delicate tendrils meshing with my essence. I pulled and the shadow wrenched her back, so I pulled harder, dragging Madeleine out of the sucking void the mutation had created inside her.

Fight… Kick, scream, thrash…

Madeleine screamed, her voice sounding far away. Her hand wrapped around my wrist and I hauled her out of the shadow with one final burst of Light, then we were hurling through the air—not literally, it seemed like something deeper than that, something almost spiritual.

Her soul, I realised. I'd just saved her soul.

We collapsed to the ground in a heap, and I wrapped my arms around her fragile frame. The mutation had taken so much out of her that I was afraid if I'd waited a second longer, the last shred of her Light would've been absorbed by the Darkness.

She sobbed, her chest heaving uncontrollably, and she clutched the front of my shirt so tight her knuckles were white.

"It's going to be okay," I murmured, smoothing her hair. "You're here. *You're here.*"

"What did she do?" Aiden asked Wilder.

"Called on Arondight," he replied.

"Arondight?"

He smiled down at me like a proud teacher, his eyes flashing silver. "She carries a shard of it inside her, you know."

19

I stood outside the Academy, looking out across the remains of last night's battle. The sky was a brilliant shade of blue and the building behind us cast long shadows across the driveway and fountain.

Wilder stood beside me, his expression grim as he stared at the blackened spot that used to be Brax's body. No one had been out with a rake to clear it away yet.

My head lolled to the side and I snapped to attention, shaking off the onset of sleep. *How embarrassing.*

"Past your bedtime?" he asked, glancing at me out the corner of his eye.

I shrugged. I'd wanted to stick by Madeleine for as long as I could. My side ached, my knee was twisted and bruised, and I sported one hell of a black eye, but the Light-infused pain meds were working a treat.

"Every time you use the shard, it wears you out, doesn't it?"

"I suppose so," I replied. "It's an enigma I need to figure out on my own. There isn't anything in the Natural handbook. I checked."

He snorted, giving away his own exhaustion.

"Do you think I did the right thing?" I asked. "Bringing her back?"

"Madeleine will be okay," he replied. "Ramona is confident she can help her."

"But she'll never be the same."

He shook his head. "Her mind is strong, but there'll always be two halves of her."

A constant battle between the demon and the Natural. I sighed, wishing I'd figured it out sooner.

"Don't sweat the what if's, Purples," he said. "You saved her soul." *But at what cost?*

"Which is more than Brax got for his troubles."

"If what that demon told you was true, then he didn't have a choice."

The One, the king of all demons, the most powerful of the horde beyond the rift. If the world was plunged into another cataclysm and he was allowed to cross… we'd all be royally screwed.

"Did I ever know the real man?" I wondered out loud.

"That's the million-dollar question everyone's asking."

Like always, more questions had been raised the moment I seemed to find answers to others. The key, the shard and the stones. The One. The existence of a rift between worlds. Things were getting… *complicated.*

"I didn't realise there were more demons back in their own world," I said. "I thought they were all here."

"So did we all, Purples."

"Something must have stopped them the first time. Closed the rift just enough so the biggest bad guys couldn't pass through."

"It would seem that way," a female voice replied.

I turned, finding Greer behind us. For such an early hour, she looked as airbrushed as ever and I felt a pang of self-consciousness over my black eye. Wilder didn't move to greet her—I wondered if it was on my account—though when he saw Madeleine being escorted out in a wheelchair, he snapped into action.

Greer and I stood together as we watched him carry Madeleine to the waiting car. There was something about him that seemed to soothe her turmoil, and while I'd taken ownership of the goth girl, I was glad she had others around her she could trust. Her road would be long and difficult, but her people wouldn't let her walk it alone.

"I find myself thanking you again, Scarlett," Greer murmured. "It seems you're full of surprises."

"Greer…" I turned, my stomach rolling, "I have to apologise to you."

She shook her head. "I have to apologise to you. I allowed my jealousy to cloud my judgment." I sucked in a sharp breath. "You're important to all of us, Scarlett. Not just for what you are, but *who* you are. Love cannot be forced or won. It just… is."

I glanced at Wilder, who was kneeling beside the

open door of the car and remembered the things I'd snapped at him last night. I'd seen them together, and while it hurt in places I'd never felt pain before, I couldn't hold it against him. The heart was a fickle thing.

I looked at Greer and found her staring at the black mark on the gravelled driveway.

"We were friends for years," she began. "Then on the council together for a decade. When I was asked to be the protector, he was the one who convinced me to bind myself to the Codex. I didn't even know…"

"It wasn't Brax," I told her. "Something had taken him over a long time ago." I didn't have to explain the rest to her.

"Yes, but for how long?"

"We can't know for certain. We can only know our own choices." She blamed herself, that much was clear, but we'd all been fooled. "The demon said he was the One."

She nodded, her eyes downcast. "Their leader. The greatest of all demons."

I supposed that was why he could use Brax's body without anyone knowing. His power was so great, he could fool us all, even the Codex.

"I'm so sorry," I said. "Brax was already gone."

"I know. I just can't help but think that we failed him. I wonder when, where… If his soul…"

"Don't," I said gently. "Don't blame yourself, Greer. We're fighting against impossible odds."

She inclined her head. "We've been forced to question everything we know and have ever been taught about demons. They're more organised, intelligent, and powerful than we gave them credit for. All this time..." She shook her head, her gaze moving to Wilder. "We haven't been fighting a war. We've been playing at one."

Now wasn't the time for defeatist attitudes. I almost had everything I needed to find the rest of Arondight, and when I did, we'd have the upper hand. Justice would be swift, and I'd go into this mysterious rift and deliver it if I had to... but it was way too early to be contemplating suicide missions.

"I have a lot to explain," I said. "I've made some... omissions in my reports."

"I suspected as much. I look forward to hearing them when I return to the Sanctum."

"You're not coming?"

"No. I want to stay and assist Liam and the students. There are a lot of frightened young Naturals inside those buildings. I'd like to offer what I can to them." She glanced at me. "I'll rejoin you at the Sanctum shortly. Ramona and Jackson are waiting."

I missed Jackson terribly, but I thought about the friends I'd made here—Trisha, Maisy, Trent, Kayla, and the rest of the seniors—and Aiden, who'd risked so much trying to help me, and knew I owed them a goodbye at least. I'd been ordered to return to London with Madeleine and Wilder, but I had unfinished business here. Besides, this was where the illustrious protector was. If anyone could shed some light on that Code page, it was Greer and Aiden. Those two needed to join forces, stat.

"I'd like to stay a few more days," I said. "There are a few things I need to finish."

"And defy your orders?" Greer asked with a half-hearted laugh. "I wouldn't expect anything less."

Inside, the Academy felt different. Maybe it was because of the battle last night, or perhaps it was the fact that this morning, Islington let me graduate early. I didn't get on the honour roll, but at least I wouldn't have to suffer through detention any more. Of course, my hasty graduation present had been the removal of my tracer.

"Scarlett!"

I turned as Trent's excited voice echoed down the hall. Everyone from the senior Light class was lingering inside the foyer. Had they been waiting to say goodbye to Madeleine? I hoped so.

"You're still here!" Trisha exclaimed.

"We thought you'd already left," Kayla added.

"How's Madeleine?" Maisy fired off.

"Is she going to be okay?" The last question was from Kayla, and I glanced at her, surprised at what seemed to be genuine concern.

"She's on her way to London," I told them. "She's very sick, and I'm not sure what'll happen, but she's in the best care."

"Do you think they'll let us visit her?" Maisy asked.

"We never got to apologise," Kayla said, "for how we treated her."

Was I hearing her right? Did I have wax in my ears? Kayla was owning up to her superior ways? She sounded sincere, and I genuinely hoped this was a permanent outlook for her.

"I know we were horrible to her," she went on. "Me most of all. We should've stuck together, no matter what."

"Madeleine's condition was no one's fault, but you're right," I said. "Together, you're stronger." *And maybe things wouldn't have been so bad.* "I don't know about visitors, but I'll put in a good word with Islington."

"You're friends now?" Trent asked with a grin.

I smirked. "Until the next time I push his buttons."

"Thanks, Scarlett," Trisha said, "for everything."

"Does that mean I'm one of the cool kids now?"

"Yeah," Kayla replied. "You're not bad… for a geriatric."

Everyone began to laugh and I joined in, warning her to watch who she called old because one day, she'd be twenty-five and realise just how *not* old that was.

As the others moved off, Trent hung back.

"Please don't ask me any more advice about girls," I told him. "I've realised I'm not equipped to be a dating guru."

He shook his head and I realised he was looking at me with something resembling awe. Great, just what I needed, a protégé. I wondered if this was how Wilder felt—exasperated and unqualified—when I followed the troll doll to that pub in London and demanded he take me to his leader.

"Seeing you fight that Colossus has kicked everyone in the arse," Trent said. "We've made a pact."

"Have you? Did you seal it with a spit handshake?"

"*Gross.*" He made a face. "No, but things are going to change around here. No more smuggling in beer and drugs and shite. Just training, so next time we can fight alongside you. Cowering in fear was a little emasculating."

"That's a big word."

"Impressed?"

"Very."

Tears prickled in my eyes and I coughed to cover up my proud mother hen moment. A year ago, I was struggling with mental illness and the boring day-to-day life of a bartender, now I was a shining example to the next generation of supernatural demon hunters. This world really was crazy.

"Remember what I told you?" I asked him.

Trent nodded. "Next time you see me, I'll have graduated. Top of the class and everything. I can't promise I'll make honour roll, though."

I laughed and shoved him playfully. "I'll hold you to that."

The library was empty when I pushed through the doors. Its familiar smells of old paper, metal, and leather filled my nostrils and I breathed deeply. I'd miss this place.

When I stood outside the office, I smiled as I saw Aiden half out of his chair and bent over his desk, pen in hand. I wasn't sure if he was asleep or just really focused on the book under his nose.

I leaned against the doorjamb and crossed my arms over my chest. Coughing loudly, I grinned as he started and almost fell off his chair.

"Scarlett! I thought you would have been on your way to London by now," he said, straightening himself.

"And I would have thought you'd be sleeping in."

He laughed softly and shook his head. "I think about books like you think about saving the world."

"Saving the world?" I quipped. "I wouldn't go *that* far, but I do like to think about swords."

His expression changed and he became thoughtful. "What you did for Madeleine…"

"Don't sweat it, teach," I declared with a wave of my hand.

"You saved her soul with a shard of Arondight."

"Seems so." I moved into the room and nudged the door closed with my boot. "Don't ask me how it works, because I'm all about trial and error."

"Imagine what you could do with all of it." He stared up at me in awe and I squirmed, uncomfortable with the attention. I didn't want a pedestal, I wanted everyone to be safe.

Sensing my awkwardness, he changed the subject. "Hey, do you still have the coin?"

"Yeah, I…" I fished around in my pocket and pulled it out.

"Do you remember how we needed a cypher to decode the page in the Codex?" I nodded as he took the coin out of my hand and turned it over. "I think it was under our noses this whole time."

"What do you mean?"

"These symbols are Druidic runes, Scarlett. The Druids were part of the Order."

"The Druids?"

"If these symbols aren't the cypher, then we're one step away from finding it."

"We've just got to figure out what they mean…"

"*Exactly*."

Too bad the last Druid had already passed on, otherwise I could have asked her. No, she wouldn't have said anything, not even for a packet of exotic seeds to add to her garden. This was a code I was meant to break on my own.

I cursed the Druids and the Naturals for their penchant for teachable moments and took the coin from Aiden. He still had his high-resolution scans on his computer.

"The Druids are gone," I said. "Is there anyone left who can read their runes?"

"Not that I know of, but it doesn't mean I'll stop trying. There's got to be links with other languages. They rarely evolve without influences from other cultures, even ones as old as ours."

I hoped he was right.

"Thanks," I said, "for everything… and I'm sorry about—"

"Don't mention it."

"Really, I—"

"I understand," he interrupted, his cheeks flushing. "I should have told you what I was doing and Madeleine…"

"Everyone missed it," I reassured him. "Even me."

He nodded but didn't look convinced. "Are you going back to London?"

"I'm hanging around for another day or so," I told him. "Greer is staying a while, too. I think you two should meet and discuss a certain Codex page. You know more about it than me."

"G-Greer?" Aiden swallowed hard and adjusted his tie from askew to slightly less askew.

"She looks like an airbrushed model from a Vogue cover, but she's not scary, I promise."

"She's fairly intimidating, you know."

I sighed. Yeah, she was.

Looking around his office, I realised I was going to miss this place. The chaos, the knowledge, the stories he'd told me about Lancelot and Genevieve. I'd even miss Galahad's gnarly suit of armour. Finally, my gaze fell on the pile of research that Islington must have returned to Aiden.

Now that things had settled some, my thoughts went to my family and lack there of.

"Hey, why did you think Andromeda could be my mother?"

"The timeline fits," Aiden replied, looking a little sheepish. Still embarrassed about his unauthorised digging, maybe? "And she bears some resemblance, don't you think?"

I picked up the photograph and studied it, tracing her features with my gaze. "I've seen her before," I murmured, "in my dreams. Or at least, I think I have."

Aiden remained silent, waiting for me to gather my thoughts.

"If she is my mum," I went on, "then that means Aldrich is my uncle." I'd really like him to be, too.

"There are ways to find out for sure," he said.

"Like a DNA test?"

"Yes, but it's Light-administered and infallible."

I sighed and returned my gaze to the photograph. "I already asked him about Andromeda. He never led me to believe that she might be my mother."

Aiden patted my shoulder. "He might not have put the same pieces together that I did."

I sniffed and went to put the photo back, but he held up his hand.

"Keep it," he said. "Just in case."

I threw my arms around his neck and held him close, breathing in his comforting scent of boy and books. He tensed but returned my embrace all the same.

I smiled, thinking about my impression of him. Aiden was nice, put together, had a great job, and I'd totally take him home to meet my parents if they were alive… but he wasn't Wilder. And Wilder wasn't someone anyone could get over in a day, let alone a few weeks.

"I'm going to go scrounge up something to eat," I said, pulling back. "Do you want to come?"

"I, uh…" he glanced at his desk, "I've got some things to tidy up here, but maybe I'll see you at dinner?"

I knew he was making up an excuse, but I didn't blame him. I would've done the same thing.

"Sure," I replied. "Sounds good."

Standing, I opened the office door.

"Scarlett, I…"

I turned, my heart skipping a beat.

Aiden smiled the smile people gave when they were letting someone go. Dull, misty-eyed, but still full of love. "Don't be a stranger, okay?"

"No," I said, my lips curving upwards, "I won't."

Looking through the windows of the infirmary, I watched Jackson as he laughed with Madeleine.

She was sitting up in bed, wires running from her chest and arms into some serious looking medical equipment. Her hand was in his and they were talking furiously about something. A debate on which console was better—PS4 or Xbox One—perhaps. That was something Jackson was passionate about, though he'd rebel and say PC, even though he competed in console-based e-sports.

I shook my head and sighed. It was good to be back in London after everything that'd happened at the Academy.

Madeleine spied me through the window and waved, drawing Jackson's attention. He glanced over his shoulder, and when he saw me, he waved me in.

"Scarlett!" Madeleine called as I walked to where she was at the end of the room. "You're back!"

"Hey," I said, standing at the foot of her bed. "I see they've got you all wired up."

"Wow, look at that shiner!" Jackson declared.

I brushed my fingers against my black eye. "Please don't remind me. At least it's fading pretty quick."

He stood and threw his arms around me, hugging me tight. "I missed you."

"Missed you to, you nerd."

"I'd watch who you're calling a nerd. I hear you graduated early and top of your class no less."

I laughed and pulled back, studying his features. "How's everything here?"

"Madeleine's doing great," he replied. "Ramona was able to halt her mutation for the time being, and it seems to be holding. There'll be some trial and error, though."

I smiled at the goth girl, who was watching us closely. "That sounds promising."

"There's been some other updates, but I'll fill you in later."

I nodded and smiled up at him. "I'm so glad to see you again, you have no idea."

He laughed and patted me on the shoulder. "Can I ask you one thing?"

"Yeah…" I gave him a look that said 'don't mess with me', but I knew he'd mess all he liked.

"Did you sort out things with Wilder?"

I choked on my spit and Madeleine stared at me wide-eyed.

"You and Mr. Wilder?" she exclaimed.

Jackson snorted. "Mr. Wilder?"

I waved him off. "It's a long story and no, there's nothing to sort. He and Greer are… Well, they rekindled, if you know what I mean."

"Really?" He narrowed his eyes. "Are you sure?"

"*Jackson.*"

"Okay, okay."

I looked at Madeleine and back to Jackson. There were a lot of things I needed to catch up on, including writing my report for Greer, but it was time for a little one-on-one girly chat.

"Jackson, would you give us a few minutes?" I nodded towards the door. "Girl talk, you know."

"Girl stuff." He shuddered, much to Madeleine's amusement. "That's my cue to va-moose."

"Va-moose?" I tilted my head to the side.

"Split," he declared, scurrying out of the Infirmary.

Laughing, I sat beside Madeleine's bed, dragging the chair closer.

"You were right," she said. "Jackson's the best."

"He's one of a kind," I agreed. "Now, how are you doing?"

She shrugged, her fingers playing with one of the wires. "I'm tired a lot. Ramona said that's the mutation fighting my Natural side."

"Have your parents arrived yet?"

"They should be here later. My dad was on a mission when they called," she explained.

"Good. I'm glad."

She squirmed, her gaze falling to her hands. "Scarlett, I'm really sorry. I never meant—"

"*Shh*," I interrupted. "There is no fault to place on anyone but the demons."

"Mr. Thompson?"

"Aiden is perfectly fine. Everyone is asking after you, you know."

She perked up. "They are?"

"Yeah, the senior class wants to come visit you."

She blew through her lips and rolled her eyes. "They just want to see the Sanctum."

"No." I took her hand in mine and squeezed. "They want to apologise for how they treated you. They want to be friends, Madeleine."

Skepticism flashed across her features, but there was also a hint of hope. "They do?"

I nodded furiously. "*They do*."

Her expression turned thoughtful and she slipped her hand out of mine. "Scarlett… Do you think I'll ever be able to go back to the Academy? If I can't be a Natural… I…" she swallowed hard, "I don't know what I'll do."

"Maybe," I replied, not knowing the answer. She might not be able to do anything if the mutation couldn't be isolated. "Right now, let's just focus on fighting this thing, okay?"

"Sure."

I stood, brushing my palms over my pants.

"Scarlett?"

"Yeah?"

"I'll never be able to thank you enough for what you did for me."

I grinned, wondering if this is what it felt like to

have a little sister. "You don't need to," I told her. "I already know."

Jackson was waiting for me out in the hall.

"You didn't have to hang around," I said, standing next to him.

"I know. I wanted to hang out with you for a bit and catch up in person for a change." He gave me a stern look. "You only sent two owls in the entire time you were away."

I laughed. "Did I hurt your pride?"

He held up his forefinger and thumb and pinched them together. "Only a little. I mean, you're so important these days."

I slapped him on the arm, my palm cracking against his bicep.

"Ow!"

We'd talked on the phone a few days after the attack. I'd filled him in on Aiden's research, the Codex page, the coin and the Order of the Twin Flames, and everything that'd happened during the fight with Madeleine's demon side. He was as up to speed as I was, though we had different paths to take after this.

He'd told me a few things about Human Convergence, too. Romy and the others had managed to track down all the humans on the list Wilder and I had found at the beta site laboratory. Only one could be saved, a woman by the name of Esme Winters, and Jackson stammered every time he'd brought her up. It was cute.

Now I was off after Arondight and the standing stones from the Codex, and Jackson was hot on the heels of the alpha site laboratory—AKA the home of Human Convergence.

"Did you ask Aldrich about Andromeda yet?"

I shook my head. "Not yet. With Greer away, he's busy and stuff…"

"I'm sure he'd make time for you."

I knew he would, but it wasn't the easiest thing to bring up. How did I tell Aldrich that I might be the daughter of his long-lost sister? Especially knowing Markzoth had murdered her and the man who I suspected was my father.

"She was the woman in my dream," I murmured. "I called her mummy with such certainty…and her arondight blade chose me. That has to mean something."

"Then ask him," Jackson said. "He already thinks of you as a daughter."

"Really? How do you know?"

"I overheard him giving Wilder a dressing down in the hall the other day. There were a few choice words if I remember correctly."

"About me? *Noooo*…" My heart lurched, and I felt the blood drain from my face. "Why didn't you tell me?"

"Because we both know how you like to over-analyse."

I slapped my hands over my face and groaned. "I'm so embarrassed."

"Don't be. Aldrich really went to town. I think his words were, *that girl is like a daughter to me. Mess with her and…* something, something." He waved a hand in the air. "You can probably guess the rest."

"Well, I appreciate the sentiment, but I already stuck up for myself."

"In spectacular fashion, I assume."

"Speaking of the constant pain in my arse, have you seen Wilder today?" Jackson smirked and I shoved his shoulder. "I said some pretty bad stuff to him and… There are a few things we need to clear up." He gave me a pointed look. "I'm trying the whole adulting thing."

"How's that working out for you?"

"*Great.*"

"Why are you asking me? I thought you always knew where he was."

"I, uh… I tuned him out," I explained. "I thought it was for the best."

Jackson's lips thinned, but he didn't ask me to elaborate. He understood better than anyone. He'd had the same kind of feelings for me and it definitely hadn't been easy for him. I still kinda felt bad about it, even though we'd well and truly worked it out.

"Have you checked the roof?"

"Not yet."

"I'd start there. He's been pouting all over the Sanctum ever since he came back. It's starting to get really annoying."

"That bodes well," I said with a roll of my eyes. "I'll catch you later."

"Good luck."

I walked through the Sanctum, taking my sweet

time. I passed the displays of weapons—the halberds, staves, and arondight hilts—and wove my way through the warren of hallways until I reached the marble foyer.

It'd been repaired in the wake of the showdown with Wainthrope and his vanguard of automatic weapons, but I could still smell the metallic scent of gunpowder. I gathered it must've been a psychological thing because someone had been through with a mop and bucket full of lemon disinfectant since then.

I stopped before the Lady of the Lake and her stone Arondight, saying a prayer before I ventured to the stairs leading to the roof.

When I opened the door, Wilder was in his usual brooding position. His shoulders were hunched, his legs dangled over the edge, and his hair was sticking up in all kinds of directions. It wasn't windy—the air was flat and stifling—so it was either laziness or frustration that'd styled him this morning.

"You're back," he said as I sat down.

"Miss me?" I teased.

"It's been oddly quiet without you around, Purples. You've got a knack for causing a scene wherever you go."

I snorted. "It's so not intentional, but at least I'm not bored."

"School's out," he quipped. "What'll you do now?"

"I suppose I'll be put to work patrolling and hunting. I'm a full-fledged Natural now," I said. "I've got a diploma and everything." I looked out over the city. "And I've got a set of standing stones to find."

"Is Aiden helping you with that?"

I nodded. "He's the man with the book smarts."

We fell into an awkward silence, and I felt our easy relationship start to slip away. This was what I was afraid of. My one-way feelings getting in the way of a rare friendship that had the potential to last the rest of our lives? Preserving it seemed more precious than romance right now.

We needed one another more than ever. Wainthrope had betrayed the Naturals at their core, the Academy had been attacked, and we'd just suffered the loss of Brax at the hands of the One. It was the most devastation we'd faced as a people since the cataclysm at Camelot.

"Scarlett, about me and Greer—"

"You don't have to explain anything. *Really.*" I swung my feet back and forth. "I said some shitty things to you and—"

"You don't have to apologise to me. I should be apologising to you."

"That'd be a first."

"I'm sorry, Scarlett."

I shrugged. "I have this mysterious destiny that doesn't really leave room in my life for much else. If we find Arondight, then I'll probably have to carry it into battle against the One, or whatever he likes to call himself. I can't sit back and let others fight the war I was destined to… Well, I don't know what I'm meant to do. That's a whole kettle of fish in itself."

Wilder grunted. "And the heart is a whole other kettle on its own."

"It wasn't meant to be," I whispered.

It didn't mean it stopped hurting. Maybe one day it would but for now, the open wound Wilder had left on my heart was still raw and bleeding. When I was with him, I'd never felt more alive. Everything was brighter in his company, and the fight against the Dark seemed worth the ultimate sacrifice if I could spend one more day with him.

But he loved another and that's just the way things were.

"Just tell me one thing," I said, staring out across the city. "Are you happy?"

"Scarlett—"

"Are you?"

His eyes flashed silver and he turned away. "I'm a work in progress."

Knowing that was the best answer I was going to get out of him, I grunted and turned back to the haze that'd fallen over central London. It was a sheen of smog, or the stink of human progress as I liked to call it.

"*The future is unwritten,*" I said, quoting the druidess.

"That's a comforting notion."

I pushed to my feet and dusted off my arse. "Well, I think we should start writing ours, don't you?"

He looked up at me with a raised eyebrow. "You want to rush into battle right now?"

"No," I said with a laugh, "don't be so dramatic. I

was thinking about starting with lunch. I hear it's
Frittata Friday."

<hr>

**Scarlett's adventure continues with DARK
GENESIS, the fourth book in the thrilling
Arondight Codex!**

*A knight in shining armour. A secret buried in time. Arondight
has never been closer to being found...*

OTHER BOOKS IN THE ARONDIGHT CODEX

by Nicole R. Taylor
series is complete!

Dark Descent #1
Dark Illusion #2
Dark Abandon #3
Dark Genesis #4
Dark Crucible #5

Continue the adventure in:
THE CAMELOT ARCHIVE

Demons, Druids, and buried secrets. The Camelot Archive is open for business.

Demon Bound #1
Demon Sworn #2
Demon Forged #3
Demon Eternal #4

ABOUT NICOLE

Nicole R. Taylor is an Australian Urban Fantasy author.

She lives in the western suburbs of Melbourne dreaming up nail biting stories featuring sassy witches, duplicitous vampires, hunky shapeshifters, and devious monsters.

She likes chocolate, cat memes, and video games.

When she's not writing, she likes to think of what she's writing next.

Follow Nicole Online:

Website: www.nicolertaylorwrites.com
Twitter: twitter.com/nicole_noir
Facebook: facebook.com/nrtaylorwrites
Newsletter: www.nicolertaylorwrites.com/newsletter
Email: nicole.this.is@gmail.com

DARK GENESIS (THE ARONDIGHT CODEX - BOOK FOUR)

A knight in shining armour. A secret buried in time. Arondight has never been closer to being found...

Scarlett Ravenwood is at a crossroads.

After suffering their biggest betrayal yet, the Naturals are on high alert. There's no telling who is on what side, or if the Light has been infected with the Dark. The end is nigh and Arondight is still out of reach.

Their only hope is a worn out coin given to Scarlett by the last of the Druids, along with a riddle no one can seem to solve. _The key, the shard, and the stones._

When Scarlett takes matters into her own hands and touches the Natural's most sacred relic, the Codex, she's shown a vision of Arondight's resting place and does what she does best—take matters into her own hands.

Her recklessness could lead the Naturals to their salvation or their doom. There's no way of telling until she puts the key into the lock and finds out what's on the other side…

Dark Genesis is the fourth novel in The Arondight Codex, an Urban Fantasy series full of adventure, mystery, and romance, woven with the spirit of heroic Arthurian legend.

Dark Genesis is OUT NOW!

www.ingramcontent.com/pod-product-compliance
Lightning Source LLC
Chambersburg PA
CBHW060808190726
48285CB00002B/593